Wagered in Winter

The Wicked Winters Book Five

By
SCARLETT SCOTT

Wedded in Winter
The Wicked Winters Book Five

ISBN: 978-1-659790-06-1

Edited by Grace Bradley
Cover Design by Wicked Smart Designs

For more information, contact author Scarlett Scott.
www.scarlettscottauthor.com

Lord Ashley Rawdon has agreed to accompany his painfully shy brother, the Duke of Coventry, to a country house party with the goal of securing him a wealthy bride. A dedicated rake, Ashley is so confident he can help his brother to ensnare the lady of his choosing, he offers him a wager. It's too bad the lady his brother selects is Miss Prudence Winter, who is infuriating, stubborn, and far too alluring.

Pru has no patience for sophisticated, handsome scoundrels like Lord Ashley. Nor does she seek a husband. All she wants is to spend the house party in peace so she can return to her charity work in London. But Lord Ashley is persistent. And far too charming.

Ashley's plan is proceeding splendidly. Until he finds himself alone with Pru, and he cannot resist stealing a kiss...

Dedication

Dedicated to Caroline Lee. I'm so honored to call you friend.
Thank you for tirelessly cheering me on!

Chapter One

Oxfordshire, 1813

*L*ORD ASHLEY RAWDON had a problem.

A tall, beautiful, brunette problem.

Ordinarily, such an obstacle would be pleasant for a man who had devoted his life to chasing, wooing, and pleasing the fairer sex. But in this situation, he was not chasing, wooing, and attempting to win the lady in question for himself.

Rather, he was attempting to do so for his brother.

There would be no delicious culmination of his efforts. He would not be taking the lovely Miss Prudence Winter's supple berry-colored lips with his. He would never help her out of her gown or find his way beneath her petticoats, and he most certainly would not know the delight of spreading her legs and plying his tongue to her cunny until she spent.

Damn and blast.

Gill was going to owe him after this.

Ash followed Miss Prudence Winter down the massive hall of Abingdon House at a discreet distance. He had no wish to cause a scandal and find himself forced into marrying the chit, after all. Even if he had always had a secret yearning for long Megs like her. And even if he found her delectably tempting.

He put the last down to his forced rustication at a country house party all in the name of helping his painfully shy brother, the Duke of Coventry, obtain a bride. Namely, one Miss Prudence Winter. She was the eldest of all the Winter sisters, wealthy ladies who hailed from trade and whose brother Devereaux Winter was doing his damnedest to use his newfound connection to nobility to ensnare aristocratic husbands for his sisters.

Hence the advent of this blasted party at Christmastide.

Hence Ash's presence in Oxfordshire.

And his current plight.

Miss Prudence disappeared into a chamber four doors down, and Ashley sped up his strides, casting a cautionary glance over his shoulder, before he, too, crossed the threshold and joined her. He found himself inside the sprawling, two-story library of Abingdon House.

Alone with the woman his brother wanted to make his future duchess.

He closed the door at his back and cleared his throat to make himself known.

Pressing a hand to her heart, Miss Prudence Winter spun about, her skirts whirling around her ankles. He fancied he caught a glimpse of slim, stocking-clad perfection and the hint of appealingly curved calves.

"What are you doing in here, my lord?" she demanded, frowning at him.

Even her displeasure was somehow alluring.

He ground his molars and forced himself to imagine a shovel's worth of cold December snow being dumped down the fall of his breeches. Anything to abate the irritating desire the disapproving creature glowering at him now inspired.

"Forgive me, Miss Winter," he said, bowing stiffly. "I find myself bored and in search of diversion. I had not realized the library was occupied."

Her lips pursed, and she raised a dark brow high, her

countenance making it apparent she did not believe him. Nor was she wrong to find him or his motives suspect. A wise woman, Miss Prudence Winter.

"Now that you realized I am within, you can see the necessity for you to go," she told him coolly.

Here was the other thing about her. Unlike most females of his acquaintance, Miss Winter was not easily won over by him. Upon their every previous interaction—three, not that he was counting—she had made him work for each word she deigned to utter.

"It would be wise for me to observe propriety and go," he agreed calmly. "However, now that I have your ear, I find myself loath to leave."

"Lord Ashley, you do not have my ear, you have my irritation," she countered, sweeping toward him with purpose in her step. "I have told you before that I have absolutely no tolerance for meaningless flattery."

Yes, she had, the impertinent baggage. Only worse.

"I believe you said you had no tolerance for meaningless flattery from empty-headed rakehells," he mused, stroking his jaw as if in deep thought.

There was no need for thought. She had said precisely that. Verbatim.

"Then one wonders why you have followed me here, Lord Ashley," she said, standing near enough now that he could touch her if he wished.

Of course, he wished.

He clenched his fists to stave off the desire.

"I did not follow you, Miss Winter," he lied.

"Of course you did," she insisted. "Just as you followed me on the two previous occasions our paths have crossed."

"Three occasions," he muttered below his breath before he could think better of it.

Ash could not be certain if she had truly forgotten how many times they had spoken or if she was intentionally nettling him. With Miss Prudence Winter, it could certainly be either.

"I beg your pardon?" she asked.

He cleared his throat again and then busied himself by brushing the sleeve of his coat. Affecting *ennui* was a special gift of his. "Nothing to concern yourself over, Miss Winter. I can assure you, I have not been following you."

She tilted her head, considering him with a chocolate-brown gaze he could not help but to feel saw far too much. "As you wish, Lord Ashley. Please just go. I am in search of a book to read. Surely there is some other lady in attendance you can attempt to seduce in my stead? I am certain I have made my lack of enthusiasm known."

Curse it, the woman was bold and brash. He would have told Gill to seek another bride, but the bind their wastrel father had left the estates in meant Gill needed to take a wife with the sort of immense funds only a Winter possessed. And the Winter sisters were all a troublesome lot, as far as Ash could tell.

Especially the Winter before him.

"You have confused the matter, I am afraid, Miss Winter," he told her calmly, forcing a polite smile. "Seducing you is not my aim at all. Rather, I am aiding my brother in his search for a bride."

She appeared distinctly unimpressed. "While offering His Grace your assistance is commendable, I fear you are wasting your time with me. I have no intention of marrying."

No intention of marrying?

Just what manner of female *was* Miss Prudence Winter?

"And why is that, Miss Winter?" he asked. "I should think marriage the goal of every eligible young lady."

Gads, he sounded like a bloody vicar. Ash shuddered inwardly.

She graced him with the smile of someone who was humoring another. "Not every eligible young lady. Indeed, some of us prefer to remain free to live our lives and spend our fortunes as we see fit."

It sounded rather a lot like his own philosophy, except he did not have a fortune. His freedom, however, yet remained his, and always would if he had any say in the matter. He was the second son. He need not marry well or at all, and spend the rest of his life a bachelor, pockets to let. There could be worse fates, surely.

Gill, however, bore all the responsibility.

"What did you have in mind for your freedom and your fortune?" he could not resist asking her, curious in spite of himself.

"I want to start my own foundling hospital," she told him.

Her response flummoxed him. He would not have been more surprised had she announced she intended to ride a donkey to the moon.

"A foundling hospital," he repeated.

"Yes." A smile curved her lush lips, so deep it revealed twin dimples in her cheeks. "My brother patronizes a foundling hospital in London, and I have thoroughly enjoyed all the time I have spent there with the children. There is nothing I would like more than to begin my own."

When she smiled like that, she was bloody breathtaking. He could not look away, even if she was spouting on about her charitable works. *Bloody hell*, the woman was a saint.

Not his sort of female, thankfully.

He preferred the licentious sort. Ladies who were selfish and interested only in finding the next vice. Ladies who were not ladies at all.

"Coventry adores children," he told her. "Indeed, it is a coincidence which cannot be overlooked that just yesterday, His Grace was telling me how desperately he longed to begin his own foundling hospital as well."

Complete rot, of course. But worth a try.

Miss Winter's lips pursed once more, her smile fading.

It was as if the summer sun disappeared behind a cloud.

Which was ludicrous. He should not even notice her smile. Or her appearance at all. She was not meant to be his. His sort of woman would have already been in his arms, long since in his bed. She would have swooned over his flattery. If she were his sort of woman, she would have had her gown around her waist, and the two of them would have been putting the oversized settee across the room to good use…or perhaps even the rug before the crackling hearth…

Devil take it, now he was sporting a stiff cock.

"Do you think me hen-witted, Lord Ashley?" she asked him, her tone more frigid than the winter air raking over the countryside beyond the Abingdon House walls.

"Of course not," he hastened to reassure her, whilst praying the fall of his coat covered the evidence of his sudden and most unwanted reaction to the fantasy of making love to her.

Not her, he reminded himself.

A fictional woman, he amended. One who was light on virtue and easy on the eyes. One who was not a chilly, disapproving long Meg with a heart as pure as an angel's. The sort he could spend all day debauching, kissing and licking every creamy curve on her body until she was writhing beneath him and crying out for more.

"Then why would you say such a thing to me?" she demanded.

His cravat was too tight. As were his breeches.

Discomfited, he slid a finger between his throat and his neck cloth, attempting to garner himself a bit more breathing room. "What is the thing in question, Miss Winter? And why are you so outraged? I cannot think a word I have spoken to you has been untoward."

He had to admit, he *had* gotten lost in his own thoughts. But he still did not think he had said anything which garnered insult. She was distracting him. For some reason, he could not bring another lady's face to mind for the fantasies he had intended to divert him from his inconvenient attraction to Miss Winter.

All he could see was her face. Her smile. Those dimples. Those soft brown eyes molten with desire. Those long legs.

Damnation.

This was not good.

Perhaps he should tell Gill he needed to find a different bride.

"You are lying to me about the Duke of Coventry's interest in foundling hospitals," she accused then. "You are an abysmal liar, my lord. Most unconvincing."

He tugged on his cravat a bit more.

Nothing about his interview with Miss Prudence Winter had proceeded as he had expected. And that, coupled with his steadily increasing desire for her, was beginning to make him incredibly vexed.

PRU HAD A problem.

Lord Ashley Rawdon was the handsomest devil she had ever seen. Tall and broad and strapping, golden-haired and godlike, he set her heart pounding whenever he appeared in a chamber. And since he had seemed to be wherever she went over the course of the last few days, she had been going about in a perpetually flustered state.

But as she watched him pulling at his elaborately knotted cravat, she began to suspect she was not the only one suffering from such an unwanted snag in the otherwise flawless fabric of her day.

He cleared his throat, looking distinctly uncomfortable. "I would never lie about such a serious matter."

She had never imagined she would find a heartless scoundrel like him appealing. But there was no denying the heat unfurling within her, nor the longing. He made her feel achy and uncertain, needy and greedy, all at once. She was heartily disappointed in herself.

Fortunately, her reaction to him could be squelched. Even if she could not control the way he made her feel—all down to his handsomeness and rakish charm, no doubt—she could ignore it.

And she *would*.

"If you are indeed trying to impress me on behalf of your brother," she told him, careful to keep her voice even and wintry, "may I at least suggest you avoid resorting to prevarications? I find your halfhearted attempts at feigning similarities between His Grace and myself most insulting."

He stopped fidgeting with his cravat then, his regard intensifying, his sky-blue eyes piercing hers. "And how would you recommend a gentleman impress you, Miss Prudence Winter?"

Heaven help her, but the way her given name rolled off his tongue made her shiver. It sent a liquid sensation straight through her, one that settled somewhere between her legs in a most improper ache.

"I cannot be impressed," she said. "But as I have already explained, I am not on the marriage mart. If, however, you are truly serious about helping Coventry to obtain a bride, you might take greater care with your manner of wooing."

He arched a brow, his lips twitching as if he suppressed his amusement. "What fault do you find with my manner of wooing?"

"For one thing, you have been following me about like a lost puppy," she said.

"I have not," he protested, true outrage in his voice.

Good, she thought unkindly. Let the beautiful scoundrel see that not every female in his presence would so quickly succumb to his rakish allure. "You most certainly have. You just did so now."

"I was bored," he clipped. "And you, Miss Winter, are impertinent."

"Honest," she corrected him. "I am being honest, Lord Ashley. I am beginning to suspect that you are a rather poor emissary for your brother to send in his stead. You have no notion of how to properly court a lady."

"I bloody well know how to court a lady." His tone, too, had grown cool. All the flattery was gone.

He had been sleepy and serpentine before, affecting boredom, spouting off nonsense. Undoubtedly, he had expected her to simply eat up every word he had said because that was how he was accustomed to being treated. Ladies likely took one look at his face, and they melted inside. She, however, was made of sterner stuff. While she could not control her body's attraction to him, she most certainly could rein in her mind and words.

"For a man who claims to know how to court a lady, you are not doing a very good job of it, are you?" she could not resist needling him. "I stand before you as evidence. No indeed, Lord Ashley. If you truly mean to help secure a bride for your brother, you must try harder."

A muscle tensed in his jaw. "What would you suggest I do, Miss Winter? Perhaps if I am as inept at courting ladies as you charge, I require some assistance."

His words gave her pause. She had not truly pondered the notion too carefully. She had been more interested in goading him than aught else. And look where she had landed herself now.

She thought for a moment, before seizing upon a reasonable way of eluding his question. "Why does your brother not do the courting himself, Lord Ashley?"

"Coventry is a man of few words," he said, unsmiling. "He is painfully shy when surrounded by those he is not familiar with, whereas I am not. He also has precious little experience with ladies. I, on the other hand, am quite familiar with the fairer sex."

For some reason, his last statement peeved her.

She was sure he was familiar with ladies. *Very* familiar. Indecently so.

"There you are," she said airily, forcing such thoughts from her mind. "That is the reason you are no good at this. You are a man who is too accustomed to wooing ladies. It has made you arrogant. Complacent, even."

He toyed with the fall of his coat, his searing gaze never leaving hers. "Arrogant and complacent, am I? Perhaps we should merely turn our minds to where I have erred. Tell me, Miss Winter, what have I done that is so wrong?"

Drat. He had routed her quite neatly. They were once more back to where they had begun, and she had no choice but to answer this time.

"We already discussed your following of me," she said.

"Like a puppy," he agreed, his tone bitter.

"Yes, a *lost* puppy," she amended. "There is also the matter of the assumption you made. You simply supposed that because I am unwed and am of marriageable age, and that your brother is a duke, I would be overjoyed to accept a proposal of marriage from him. However, you were vastly wrong, were you not?"

His lips twitched again. "It would seem I was. Thankfully, I have you to show me the error of my ways."

"Yes," she agreed. "Furthermore, if you wish to court a lady, the best way to do so is not by plying her with lies. Instead, you should attempt to woo her in other ways. Dance with her. Discuss what she likes to read. Make her laugh. That sort of thing."

There. He could hardly find fault with that, could he?

"Indeed, Miss Winter," he said. "These are all excellent suggestions, and they rather have me thinking that perhaps a bargain of sorts is in order."

"A bargain?" A tiny seed of misgiving burrowed itself into her heart.

Bargains with rakes only ever led to trouble, she was sure of it.

"Yes," he said smoothly. "Since you have no intention of marrying, and since you have such a plethora of ideas for ways I may become a more successful proxy suitor for my brother, it is only fair that you tutor me."

She should tell him no. Immediately.

And yet, she was curious. "What would I receive in return, Lord Ashley? It is a bargain, is it not?"

He flashed her a blinding grin she felt all the way to her toes. "You have my promise to volunteer for one day at your foundling hospital after you have opened it."

"One day is not enough," she decided instantly. "How about a fortnight?"

"A sennight," he countered.

"Done," she said.

He bowed to her once more, and the seed of misgiving began to sprout. He looked pleased, the devilish man.

"I look forward to commencing our lessons, Miss Winter."

Good heavens. What had she done?

Chapter Two

*A*SH REINED IN his mount, drawing the mare to a walk alongside his brother's gelding. The December air was unnaturally cold this year, making a simple pleasure like riding a rather unenviable jaunt. It was one of the only ways, however, he and Gill could garner even a moment alone to speak to each other candidly.

"How goes the wooing?" he asked pointedly, for he had not forgotten the manner in which he had reluctantly become his brother's romantic emissary.

Frustrated by Gill's lack of progress at even managing a simple tête-à-tête, Ash had made a wager with him that he alone could make any lady of Gill's choosing amenable to marrying him. Gill, blighter that he was, had chosen Miss Prudence Winter. Who also happened to be the lone lady of the gathering who had captured Ash's interest, even prior to the ill-fated bet.

"No wooing," said Gill, with his usual brevity.

They were one year apart in age, and as the heir and the spare, they had been raised together. Both had been the recipients of their father's cruelty and capriciousness. The former Duke of Coventry had been not just a wastrel but a drunkard, and when deep in his cups—which had been nearly every day—he had been particularly brutal to Gill. And Gill had simply retreated to a place inside himself no one else could reach. Social settings such as this one proved especially difficult for him.

Though he had mastered his reactions to the point of appearing blank and cold, Ash knew how much large gatherings and forced interactions affected his brother. Sometimes, the old ghosts returned with crippling vengeance, and Gill could scarcely even utter a word.

Ash had grown accustomed to speaking for him.

As someone who had spent most of his life in his brother's shadow—the spare only—he had perfected the art of being noticed. Which was proving a boon for Gill, who needed to snag an heiress with an impossibly fat dowry, *yesterday*. That was, if he meant to save the vast Coventry holdings.

Which, of course, they both did. And that reminded him.

"You have yet to speak with Miss Prudence Winter?" he prodded.

Gill sighed, his breath puffing into a silver cloud on the icy air. "I have not."

"Have you spoken with any of the females at this curst house party?" Ash asked, suspecting he already knew the answer.

Gill had thus far successfully avoided most of the drawing room games where he might reasonably exchange words with one of the ladies. No Hoodman Blind or Bullet Pudding for the Duke of Coventry, for fear he would be forced to speak or make eye contact with a mere acquaintance.

Their soulless father had scarred Gill all too well.

"One," Gill admitted, his blue stare trained on the horizon.

"Not Miss Prudence, however," Ash mused. "It was not a maid, was it? You cannot count interaction with a female if she is a servant."

"Servants are people," Gill gritted.

The former Duke of Coventry had not believed so. To him, servants had been vessels for his rage, for his lust. For his verbal lashings. They had existed to serve him, and they should have been pleased to do it.

"Of course they are," Ash agreed, "but you cannot very well marry a maid, now can you? Therefore, she does not count."

"I could," his brother countered tersely.

"A maid with a dowry as large as one of the Winter ladies'?" Ash hiked a brow and gave an incredulous laugh. "No such female exists."

"It was not a maid," Gill admitted, frowning.

Promising, he supposed. Unless the lady was already wed. Or not nearly plump enough in the purse…

The suspense irked him. He had been chasing after Miss Prudence Winter at his brother's behest, and all in the name of their wager, and yet Gill had spoken to a female. "Who was it then?"

"Miss Christabella Winter," Gill allowed, not a hint of inflection entering his tone.

Of all the Winters, the flame-haired, garrulous one would have been Ash's last guess.

"The troublesome chit?" he asked.

"She does not seem troublesome," Gill said, his tone going a trifle defensive.

Interesting.

"Red-haired?" Ash clarified. "Always chattering?"

"She caught me having one of my spells," Gill admitted, shame tingeing his voice.

The devil. He had been hoping his brother would have fared better at this extended country house party than he had at other events in the past, in part because Ash had accompanied him there.

"Where were you when it happened?" He hated that after all these years and their bastard of a father's death, Gill was still haunted by the ghosts of the past.

"Hiding in a blasted salon," Gill said.

Damn.

"Where was *I* when it happened?" he asked, for aside from the time he had spent pursuing Miss Prudence Winter on his brother's behalf, he had done his best never to stray from Gill's side.

"Skirt chasing?" Gill asked, his tone pointed.

"I have not been chasing any skirts here." He glowered at his brother. "Which is probably why I am all but going mad with restlessness. Have you any idea how long it has been since I have last had a woman?"

So bloody long that Ash himself could not even recall. Thank the Lord this house party would not last beyond the next fortnight. Any longer, and he would perish.

"You will survive," Gill said mildly. "I have survived eight-and-twenty years thus far."

Yes, much to Ash's horror, his brother was a damned virgin. Not for Ash's lack of attempting to help his brother to rectify that sin. He had once enlisted the aid of London's most desired courtesan. And not even she had managed to break through Gill's walls.

An utter waste, for Ash had wooed her himself, and yet had not been able to reap the rewards of his diligence. They shared blood. There was no way in hell they would ever share women.

Which was what made Ash's unwanted lust for Miss Prudence Winter so very disturbing. And wrong. And as fruitless as a winter's garden. Because nothing could be done about it, especially if she was to become his brother's wife.

The very thought of Miss Prudence Winter becoming the

next Duchess of Coventry was enough to make him want to gag.

"How you have managed to survive that long remains one of life's innumerable mysteries," he forced himself to say. "I do not have your fortitude. But even so, you know very well that my sole purpose in coming here was to aid you in securing the bride you need."

"Yes," agreed Gill, "and I am grateful for your concern as ever, Brother. Tell me, have you made any progress with Miss Prudence Winter?"

"I rather think I have," he said grimly. A change of subject was desperately needed. "But enough of that. Race me to the tree line? On the count of three. One…two…three!"

They kicked their mounts into a gallop in unison, and as they soared toward the centuries-old trees on the edge of the field, the winter's wind buffeting them, Ash told himself he was doing the right thing.

For all the right reasons.

MUCH TO HER shame, Pru was hiding from Lord Ashley Rawdon.

She was ensconced in a small salon in the far west wing of Abingdon House where she was certain no one would find her, curled up on an overstuffed chair. And she was reading a book. Not just any book, as it happened. A rather wicked book. One of a series that Christabella had managed to acquire with the help of her enterprising lady's maid.

The Tale of Love was the name, and the words, like the forbidden engravings, were wicked. Bawdy. Shocking. If their overly protective brother Dev ever discovered his sisters were not only in possession of one of the most lurid and sensational series of novels recently published but had been consuming it quite thoroughly from frontispiece to the last page, his rage would have no end.

The Tale of Love was written in the form of a series of letters between two dear friends, regaling each other with ribald tales of *on dits* and their own sensual escapades. Each letter discussed the forbidden in great, shocking detail. As a lady who had been largely shielded from such matters, Pru had an insatiable curiosity for the truth.

But as riveted as she had often been to the pages of the books, for some reason, she could not seem to concentrate upon the words before her now. Her mind continued to wander to a golden-haired, blue-eyed rakehell who had cozened her into promising to teach him how to court ladies.

Ladies such as herself, she supposed.

Not that she wanted Lord Ashley to court her. Or that she wanted any man to court her, for that matter. She was happy enough with her future plans laid. She would build her own foundling hospital from the ground up. She most certainly had no intention of becoming anyone's wife. And she most certainly had no need to teach Lord Ashley Rawdon anything.

Except that she had struck a bargain with him. And her honor would not allow her to forget it. Instead, she had spent the past two days since he had found her in the library outmaneuvering him at every turn. If he moved nearer to her in a crowded room, she shied away. She made certain she had a partner at the ready for every drawing room game. She broke her fast in her chamber. She took great care when sneaking into chambers for some much-needed time alone.

Just as she had done today.

The door to the salon opened abruptly, jarring her from her troublesome thoughts.

And, as if conjured by her wayward introspections—or

perhaps even by her acidic guilt—there he stood. Tall, more beautiful than any man ought to be, a knowing grin already on his lips. He moved with the lithe sophistication only a true rakehell could perfect. As if he knew every pair of feminine eyes within reach would devour the sight of him, from his well-muscled horseman's thighs clad in those form-fitting breeches to his broad shoulders and the immaculate cut of his coat.

Because they were.

Because he was Lord Ashley Rawdon, and he was handsome as sin.

Tempting as the devil.

She sighed.

He bowed.

The door closed behind him, leaving the two of them perfectly, improperly, alone.

"Miss Winter," he greeted. "How startled I am to find you here."

The liar.

She rose and dipped into a curtsy because she knew she must, but as she did so, she hid the book carefully behind her back. For if anyone would know *The Tale of Love* upon sight, surely it would be he.

"You are back to following me again, I see, Lord Ashley," she observed coolly.

"On the contrary, my dear," he returned, his tone smooth and unflappable as his mien, "I have never been following you. Fortune's wheel has merely given me an excellent turn a time or two."

"Or four," she could not help but to point out, even if she was being rude.

"Ah, now the lady can count." He winked at her and strode nearer in a casual fashion, as if he had all day to approach her. "What are you hiding behind your back, Miss Winter?"

Of course, he had noticed. She did not think there was a thing Lord Ashley Rawdon missed. The man was dreadfully observant for an indolent rakehell. But then again, she was beginning to think she had mistaken him. For though he was a charming rogue, there was nothing indolent about him.

"I am hiding nothing, my lord," she said calmly, though her hands clenched the book in a tighter, more protective grip behind her back. "For I have nothing to hide."

"Indeed?" He stopped when he was near enough to touch.

So close she could detect the odd striations of color in his irises. Violet and gray with a hint of sea green.

She would have taken a cautionary step backward, but the chair she had so recently vacated would not allow it.

"Indeed," she bluffed, hating the way her voice emerged. Breathless. Affected.

Because he *did* affect her, and much to her dismay, the affliction he caused whenever she was in his presence was only growing worse.

He held out a hand. Ungloved. "Then you will not mind sharing your reading selection with me. I confess, I am curious as to what sort of book would cause Miss Prudence Winter to hide herself away in a far-flung salon."

The sight of his bare hand should not make her heart race. Nor should the scent of him—lemon tinged with musk—send heat pooling between her thighs. The scent of his cologne was as bright and alluring as he was. It suited him, she thought.

But she was not giving him the book.

Not now.

Not ever.

"I fear you would find my choice of reading horridly

boring," she managed to say. "Why did you seek me out again today, my lord? Perhaps you are here for your lessons?"

"Lessons."

The way he repeated the lone word was scandalous.

It echoed between her thighs in a wanton ache.

How could one man make such an innocuous word sound so wicked?

"Courting lessons," she elaborated.

Not whatever lessons he implied. However enjoyable and forbidden and tempting they may be.

"Now that I am here, we may as well begin," he said, stroking his jaw as if contemplating something colossal. He wiggled the fingers of his outstretched hand. "But first, the book, if you please. It is horridly unkind of you not to share the reading tastes of a lady with me."

Drat him, why did he have to fixate upon the book? It was as if the man possessed a secret window into her mind. He seemed to know that she wanted to keep him as far away from *The Tale of Love* as possible. Meanwhile, he wanted to get his hands upon it. Thinking of his hands made her glance down, once more, to his outstretched palm and long, elegant fingers. When had a gentleman's hand ever made her knees go weak? And why could she not look upon them without imagining them touching her...

Gliding over her bare skin in the whisper of a decadent caress...

Oh, dear. Her cheeks went hot. Perhaps she had been reading Christabella's wicked books for too long. She was growing fanciful. And foolish.

She cleared her throat. "It is a volume of poetry. I hardly think you would find it of interest."

"I adore poetry." This time, he flashed her a grin.

He was *enjoying* this, the knave.

"Here is your first lesson," she snapped. "Do not harass a lady over her reading choices. Perhaps she does not want to share. Perhaps she recognizes the importance of leaving a bit of mystery to everything."

"Does this rule apply to all ladies, or just you, my dear Miss Winter?" he asked.

"It certainly applies to me," she told him airily, "though I cannot speak for all other ladies. Certainly, forcing a lady to do anything against her will is strictly against the rules of proper courting."

"On that we are in agreement." His expression, like his tone, had turned solemn. His eyes searched hers. "But there is always persuasion, is there not?"

He stepped nearer.

She emitted a most unladylike squeak. He was close enough to kiss now. Not that she wanted to kiss him. Her gown was billowing into his legs. How tall he was, she thought again. She was accustomed to looming over most gentlemen, but not Lord Ashley. He stood at least half a head taller than she.

"Persuasion?" she asked, then shook her head so vehemently the hair framing her face swept into her eyes. "Persuasion is not part of the rules of courtship, my lord."

She blinked, but the dratted curls her lady's maid had fashioned that morning remained lodged to her eyelashes, impeding her sight.

Until Lord Ashley moved suddenly, using his outstretched hand to brush the curls from her eyes. The pads of his fingertips grazed her cheek. The touch—nothing more than the mere glance of his skin against hers—sent a bolt of white-hot desire straight to her core. The place where he had touched her tingled. Every part of her felt alive.

Their gazes met once more, and this time, they held.

"In my experience, persuasion is one of the most enjoyable forms of wooing a lady," he said, his voice low.

The glorious rumble of it settled over her.

"What manner of persuasion?" she dared to ask.

Even though she knew such a question was foolhardy.

Even though she knew better than to pose such a question to a man like Lord Ashley Rawdon.

He was trouble, after all.

"This is the sort of thing better demonstrated than explained, I find," he said then, and his gaze had dipped to her lips. "Shall I?"

She thought, quite uselessly, that she would have said yes to anything he asked with that molten stare of his upon her, his scent filling her senses, his large, strong form towering over her. He made her feel feminine. Feminine and desirable.

Dangerous combinations.

"That will not be necessary," she forced herself to say. "I am sure I can surmise, Lord Ashley. Now, if you do not mind, please be kind enough to grant me some space. The second lesson of proper courting is that you ought to observe the proprieties at all times."

She said the last as much to remind herself as to remind him.

But it would seem it did her little good. For in the next instant, she found herself wrapped in his arms.

"To hell with propriety," he growled. "Allow me to show you the finer art of persuasion, Miss Winter."

And then, his mouth touched hers.

Chapter Three

$\mathcal{H}$ E WAS KISSING Miss Prudence Winter.
 The woman his brother had chosen as his future duchess.

And *damn*, what a muddle. He would never be able to look upon her without recalling the soft give of her lips beneath his. Without knowing how she tasted—of hot chocolate and everything forbidden. Without remembering how good her body felt in his arms—all lithe curves, long legs, and sinful woman.

But her mouth was pliant and warm beneath his. The fire ignited in his blood was undeniable. And although he knew he was casting a dark mark upon his soul, he could not stop. One of his hands cupped her face, the silken skin of her cheek burning into him like a brand. The other had settled upon her waist, drawing her more firmly against him.

This kiss was unlike any other he had ever experienced. She had opened for him instantly, on a sweet sigh of surrender. A sigh that echoed straight through him. Though he was not a man given to maudlin sentiment, he could not shake the notion that this moment, this woman, this kiss had been meant to be. He had never been overwhelmed by mere kisses before.

But he was now. Everything was Prudence Winter: the sweet smell of a sunlit garden in bloom, the sound she made when his tongue slid deeper into the honeyed depths of her mouth, the warmth and vibrancy of her beneath his hands.

Ash had a new problem.

An even bigger problem than Miss Prudence Winter.

He could not stop kissing her. His sense of honor attempted to intervene. He was dimly aware of the sound of something thudding to the floor. Perhaps the book she had been so bloody determined to keep from him? He forgot to care when, in the next moment, her arms wound around his neck.

She pressed herself closer, her breasts crushing into his chest. And she kissed him back. Kissed him as if she were starved for him. Her tongue moved against his. The fusing of their mouths turned carnal. His cock strained against the fall of his breeches, and every part of him thundered with a rare and raw desire so visceral, his ballocks tightened.

Good God, he had been right when he had told Gill he had gone too long without a woman.

Damnation.

Gill.

His brother.

His brother who wanted to marry the woman in Ash's arms. The woman whose mouth he was currently ravishing.

Guilt slammed into Ash. He forced himself to end the kiss. To lift his head.

Miss Prudence Winter's gaze was glazed. Her berry-red lips were swollen and darker, marked by their shared kisses. Her slack countenance was an ode to passion. Lust hit him like a runaway horse, wild and uncontrollable. Everything in him was roaring for more.

But he was also disgusted with himself.

What had he done?

How could he kiss his brother's future bride? And, worse,

how could he secretly long to lift her skirts and take her for his own? How could he long for her with such desperation, his body ached, and he was closer than a hairsbreadth to discarding the last shred of his restraint and taking her maidenhead before his brother could?

He swallowed down a knot of bile and forced a feigned smile to his lips. "There you are, Miss Winter. Persuasion."

He did his best to pretend the kiss had not just altered everything he knew about himself. As if he did not want to do it again. And again. And again. As if he did not find her maddeningly tempting and utterly delicious. As if the only honor he had believed himself to possess—loyalty to his brother—had just fled.

"You ought not to have done that," she murmured, her voice sounding unsteady.

On that, they were in complete accord, he thought grimly.

"Forgive me," he managed to say. "That was unconscionable of me. I was attempting to return the favor of your lessons, and I got…carried away by the moment."

Carried away was putting it mildly. What a blighter he was.

She did not offer her answer immediately.

Ash forced himself to turn his attention to something else—anything—aside from the kisses he had just shared with Miss Prudence Winter. Instead, he seized upon the notion of the book, which had dropped at some point during their mad kisses. He stepped back, releasing her, and adjusted his coat to make certain it fell over his straining cockstand before lowering his gaze to the floor.

He spied the book instantly. When it had fallen, it cracked open, leaving two pages on display. And on the pages was an engraving. He sank to his haunches, reaching for it as shock lanced through him.

Along with a renewed surge of desire.

Surely his eyes were deceiving him. Prim and proper Miss Prudence Winter, unmarried, innocent lady who spouted off about foundling hospitals, would not be reading *The Tale of Love*. Would she?

The series of books had recently been published to great scandal. They were bawdy and wickedly descriptive. Illustrated with explicit engravings of sexual acts. Acts no innocent should see.

But the innocent lady in question was hastier than he was. She snatched the volume from the floor and snapped it closed before he could confirm it was indeed an engraving of a man performing cunnilingus.

There were, however, certain sights a man could recognize from across a bloody chamber. Coitus of any sort was one of them, even if it was represented in black and white engravings upon a leather-bound page.

She held the volume to her breast in a protective gesture as she rose to her feet once more. The pink in her cheeks, already present from their shared kisses, blossomed to an even deeper shade.

He rose to his full height, towering over her, the taste of her on his lips. That mouth of hers still called to him, and he could not help but think of all the filthy things he could do with it. To it. Slide his—

Nay.

He banished the thought.

Think of the book, he told himself. *Think of Gill. Think of all the estates which will fall into further ruin and be sold off if Gill does not acquire his wealthy Winter bride.*

And then, a new emotion hit him. Outrage. His brother deserved better in his duchess than a woman who would allow his own brother to kiss her. A woman who was, even now, likely in possession of one of the filthiest books printed in the English language.

"Tell me, Miss Winter," he said cuttingly, "is reading bawdy literature a part of proper courting?"

Her cheeks went ashen, her knuckles going white over the book. How he wished he could see the cover, but she was doing a fair job of denying him any telling view.

"It most certainly is not, Lord Ashley," she snapped, finding her voice at last. "Nor is forcing kisses upon the ladies you are intending to court."

Forcing kisses?

Oh, no she had not.

"I believe I must have misheard you, Miss Winter," he said, warning in his tone.

He was Lord Ashley Rawdon. He did not force ladies into anything. Nor did he have to. Ladies fell into his lap and into his bed and onto his cock quite of their own free will, and with regularity, too.

"You heard me correctly," she said, chin going up, her countenance suddenly one of supreme defiance. "If you think I wanted you to kiss me, or if you think I liked it, you are wholeheartedly wrong. Rakes do not impress me, Lord Ashley. They never have."

Before he could say another word to that, the door to the salon swept open, and there stood none other than his brother. *Oh, hell.* This had just gone from bad to abominable with all haste.

PRU HELD *THE Tale of Love* to her as if it were a shield as she stared between Lord Ashley and the Duke of Coventry. Had they planned this? Surely not, for if Lord Ashley was indeed attempting to investigate the merit of possible brides for his brother, why would he go about kissing them himself first?

And the duke looked shocked to find the chamber inhabited.

When his gaze lit upon Lord Ashley and Pru, he bowed elegantly, but said nothing.

It was the treatment Pru had come to expect from Coventry. She did not think she had seen him speak more than ten words since his arrival at Abingdon Hall.

"Coventry," said Lord Ashley, bowing back at his brother as if he had not just destroyed Pru with those kisses, only to treat her with such icy scorn.

A contradiction, this man. He kissed her with fire and passion, kindling the spark within her into an uncontrollable flame, and then simply stopped. It was as if she had seen two versions of him. Both left her reeling and unsure of herself.

She dipped into a curtsy, her ears going hot. "Your Grace."

Coventry did not meet her gaze. Instead, he appeared frozen. He was stiff, his countenance pale. She wondered if it was because of the shocking disregard for propriety she and Lord Ashley had evinced, alone together in the salon, unchaperoned.

And then she wondered if perhaps he had been a witness to the kiss.

Lord Ashley was striding to his brother's side, his countenance etched with worry. "Gill?" he said quietly. "What is it?"

His pleasant baritone carried to her, sending an unwanted frisson down her spine.

She did not want to be affected by the tall, dashing rake. And yet, she was. It was irrefutable. Not that she would ever admit as much to *him*.

She seized upon the opportunity to flee, giving the brothers their privacy. Something was clearly amiss with Coventry, though she did not dare guess what. Holding her book tightly to her, she rushed toward them both, the need to escape propelling her forward.

"If you will excuse me, Lord Ashley, Your Grace," she managed to say with remarkable poise, considering she had just been kissed senseless by one of them and then caught in possession of a wicked book. "I was leaving when Lord Ashley came upon me here."

"Yes," Lord Ashley said, eying her in a way she could not like. "Go, Miss Winter. Run."

She was not running, she told herself as she slipped past the brothers—Coventry still standing like a statue not far from the threshold—and made her way into the hall. The door closed at her back, and she gathered her skirts in both hands, taking care to hide the book within the voluminous fall of her gown. And then she hastened her pace, eager to put as much distance between herself and Lord Ashley Rawdon as possible.

Indeed, her feet were moving at such a pace, that when she rounded a bend in the hall, she collided with someone traveling in the opposite direction with equal speed. The someone turned out to be her sister, Christabella. They caught each other's arms, steadying one another to keep from falling.

Pru took in her sister's flushed countenance, along with the disheveled state of her hair.

"Christabella, what has happened?" she demanded instantly.

Her sister looked as if she had just been properly ravished. There was no other way to describe it. Her expression was dazed. Fat tendrils of brilliant red hair had come loose from her coiffure, spilling to her shoulders. She was missing more than one hair pin, that much was certain. Pru's protective sisterly instincts flared to life.

"Nothing has happened," her sister said at last, blinking. "Pru? What are you doing in this wing? I thought it rather uninhabited."

As had Pru, which was why she had come here to hide from Lord Ashley. At the realization, her eyes narrowed.

Pru knew it was her duty to ask the obvious. "Have you just come from an assignation, Miss Christabella Mary Winter?"

Christabella's already flushed cheeks deepened to a shade of scarlet to rival her hair. "No," she denied quickly.

Too quickly. Far, far too quickly. Of all the Winter sisters, Christabella was the wildest. She was also the romantic of the five of them. Determined to land a rake at all costs. Pru herself was far too practical to ever find herself wooed and seduced by such a man. Lord Ashley included.

"You were meeting with someone," Pru pressed, concern for her sister prodding her to seek answers. "Tell me the truth."

Christabella's gaze swept past Pru, to a point over her shoulder. "Of course I was not. I was merely seeking out some solitude. You are the one who practically knocked me off my feet. Where were you fleeing to in such haste?"

Pru's own guilt ate at her, but she forced it down, telling herself she would fret over her actions later. What she had before her now was plain evidence that her sister had been potentially ruined.

"What happened to your hair?" she demanded. "It looks as if a man has been running his fingers through it."

Christabella's hands flew to her hair, tentatively inspecting the damage. "Perhaps I lost a hair pin. I was outside in the garden earlier, and it is quite windy."

That was a lie, and Pru could see it plainly.

"The wind did not steal a hair pain," she countered grimly, "and from the looks of it, you are missing more than one pin. I would wager at least five are gone, if not more."

Christabella patted her hair. "Perhaps it is from my bonnet, then. It did get caught in my hair when I was removing it."

"Why do you not tell me the truth?" she countered. "I am not a fool. I have eyes in my head. Your gown is wrinkled. Why, your skirts look as if they have been crushed."

Good God, had Christabella been completely compromised in every sense of the word?

"I fell in the gardens," her sister told her.

"Why is your gown not dirty?" she asked.

"Because there is snow in the gardens." Christabella smiled, pleased with herself, it would seem, for the quick fashion in which she had arrived at the excuse.

An unusually early winter's storm had indeed blanketed the land in a dense coating of white. But Pru was sure the truth of what had befallen her sister had nothing to do with a garden, wind, or a fall. At least, not one into snow. A fall into the arms of a wicked man, however…

"You expect me to believe your hair was ruined by the wind," she said, frowning at her defiant sister. "That the wind not only pulled your hat from your hair, but that it also plucked a handful of pins from it. And that after you were so mauled by the wind, leaving your hair half-unraveled down your back, you proceeded to fall into the snow in such a manner that your gown became hopelessly wrinkled. Much in the same fashion it would become wrinkled if it were raised to your waist?"

Christabella eyed her mulishly. "And how would you know what such wrinkles would look like, Pru? I confess, I

32

cannot determine the difference between wrinkles caused by a Biblical fall and wrinkles caused by a literal fall. But if you can do so, pray, enlighten me."

Christabella was being remarkably stubborn and resilient in her refusal to admit to what had happened. Ordinarily, that was not the way of it with the more outspoken of the Winter sisters.

Something horrid occurred to Pru then, out of nowhere.

Horrible.

Awful.

Unthinkable.

There was only one other rake running about this wing of Abingdon House. And Pru had just left him behind. After he had owned her lips with his. But surely Lord Ashley would not be such a despicable cad, such a relentless blackguard, such a devious, heartless scoundrel, that he would despoil one sister and then another within the span of an hour?

Would he?

Her chest tightened at the thought.

The man was a rake. Handsome as sin. His reputation preceded him. Was there not the rumor about him having three paramours at once? How had she forgotten? She had believed she was made of sterner stuff than to simply allow herself to be so thoroughly seduced by a silver tongue and a wicked smile.

A question she did not want to pose rose within her. She had to ask.

"Did Lord Ashley Rawdon ravish you?" she demanded of Christabella, sick at the notion.

Christabella frowned at her. "Why should Lord Ashley want to ravish me?"

Her confusion appeared genuine. Relief slid through Pru. She liked to think she knew her sister well enough to discern between the truth and a lie.

"If it was not Lord Ashley, then who was it?" she asked.

"No one ravished me," Christabella denied. "Truly, Pru. Did you not hear a word I just said? I was in the gardens—"

"Tell me the truth, Christabella, and tell me now," Pru interrupted, growing weary of their back and forth.

Christabella heaved a dramatic sigh. "Very well. I shall tell you, but you must promise not to go to our brother with this."

"I promise," Pru said easily. "Now out with it."

"It was the Duke of Coventry," Christabella said softly. "But he did not ravish me. Not at all. I was helping him."

Pru's brows rose, shock coursing through her. She would not have been more surprised had her sister announced she had just returned from a trip to the moon. "Coventry?"

"Yes," her sister said, looking a bit shame-faced at the admission.

Pru shook her head. "The Duke of Coventry? The man who scarcely speaks? *He* is the one who ravished you?"

"Hush!" Christabella cast a glance over her shoulder, her expression turning guilty. "Not so loud, if you please. Yes, it was he. But he did not ravish me, Pru. I swear it."

Pru eyed her sister, foreboding blossoming inside her. "You had better tell me everything, Christabella Mary Winter. Start at the beginning."

Chapter Four

$\mathcal{G}$UILT WAS A monster with gaping maws, threatening to swallow him whole. But Ash would be damned if he would allow it. All he needed was distraction. Distraction accompanied by a dash of brandy.

Instead of brandy and distraction, he found Miss Prudence Winter.

In the library. It was half past one in the morning, and the moon was a silver glow in the brilliant blackness of the night sky. No one was supposed to be about. He had thought the entire company was abed.

The glow beneath the door had warned him, as he had approached, that he would not be alone. But he had entered anyway, thinking instead to find another gentleman within, similarly seeking to find solace in their host's book collection and brandy stores. Yet, the figure, illuminated by a lone brace of candles settled upon a table within, could not be mistaken.

Her back had been turned but at his entrance, she whirled about to face him, her dark hair unbound and tumbling down her shoulders. *Lord God*, she was wearing nothing more than a virginal nightdress with a dressing gown belted atop it. His mouth went dry.

He forgot how to speak.

Miss Prudence Winter, however, suffered from no such affliction.

"Lord Ashley," she snapped, irritation quivering in her lush voice. "Is that you?"

What the devil sort of greeting was that? He ought to be insulted. He could recognize her easily in the darkness. Indeed, he was reasonably certain he would know her anywhere, even in nothing but the moonlight with no candle at all to illume the way.

Especially in the moonlight, said the wickedest part of him.

His prick was already twitching to life.

He moved toward her, drawn as the bee to a blossom.

"It is indeed I, Miss Winter," he said, happy to see her in spite of himself.

Though mere hours had passed since he had seen her at dinner, and only a scant few more hours before that when he had been alone with her in the salon—when he had kissed her—he was pleased to see her once more now. Genuinely pleased. And not because he wanted to kiss her again, or because she had been the source of his every morning cockstand since his arrival at Abingdon Hall—which she most certainly had—but because he found her company enjoyable. He liked the dulcet sound of her voice. He liked her flashing eyes and her quick wit. He even enjoyed the way she eviscerated him with her sharp tongue.

A tongue he wished he could put to other uses, it was true.

Blast, he really must think of something else now…

"Have you followed me yet again?" she demanded, sounding outraged.

Not this time, he could have said.

"I am innocent of all charges laid against me," he told her instead, grinning.

Damn it, he had to stop this. Because he had already

kissed her. And he could not do so again. Not when Gill was still intent upon taking her as his bride. He never had discovered what had been bothering his brother earlier in the day. Thankfully, Gill had not suspected what Ash had been about.

They had chatted about horseflesh. The intolerable cold. The ladies in attendance.

Gill had once more expressed his belief that the eldest Winter would make an excellent duchess. And the point could not be argued. She was lovely, calm, and handled herself with ladylike aplomb. Except for the matter of her kissing other gentlemen and secreting bawdy books…

But he hadn't had the heart to bring up the subject with Gill. And as a result, the guilt was only growing more pronounced by the moment. Rivaling Ash's lust.

What a pathetic arse he was.

"I daresay you have not been innocent since you were a babe," Miss Winter countered.

She was not wrong.

He pressed a hand to his heart, as if she had wounded him. "I am insulted, Miss Winter, that you think so ill of me. Particularly when you are no angel yourself."

Her eyes widened as he strode even nearer, not stopping until he could touch her. He could so easily draw an arm around her waist and pull her against him. But he did not.

"What are you suggesting, Lord Ashley?" she asked.

"Call me Ash," he invited. "All my familiars do."

Her lips pursed as if she had just tasted something sour. "I am not your familiar."

"You were quite familiar earlier," he reminded her, although he knew he should not.

For both their sakes. This mad flirtation would have to come to an end. As would his equally mad desire for her.

"You were the one who was familiar," she snapped back. "Too familiar, if you will recall. Your advances were improper."

He grinned. "Improper advances are the only kind I prefer to make."

The guilt was still there, festering beneath the surface of their every interaction. Reminding him this was dangerous territory. But he could not help himself when it came to this woman. She was intoxicating.

"You are a rake and a scoundrel, Lord Ashley," she said, but the sting was absent from her words.

She sounded, instead, intrigued.

"Ash," he prodded, making the mistake of reaching out and taking up a tendril of her hair. Because it was silken in his fingers. And he could not let it go, nor could he stop thinking about wrapping it around his fist. Running his fingers through it.

Damnation.

"Lord Ashley," she said again, emphasizing the formality.

Just as well, he supposed. He forced himself to release that seductive lock of her hair. "Miss Winter," he returned, then reminded himself of the bawdy book. "Were you, or were you not, reading a bawdy book earlier when I came across you in the salon?"

"I was reading poetry," she denied.

He admired the way the candlelight played over her features, softening them. "Poetry books are not often accompanied by engravings, are they, my dear?"

"Engravings?" There was an edge to her voice.

Guilt, he thought.

"When your book fell to the floor, it opened to a certain page," he elaborated. "I did not mistake what I saw."

"Why are you not abed, Lord Ashley?" she asked, clearly

changing the subject. "Why are you continuously wherever I am?"

"Would you believe I am searching for my lessons in proper courtship?" he teased. "I could not sleep for wondering what the next lesson would be and when I could receive it."

"Now is as good a time as any, my lord," she said coolly. "If you are attempting to court a lady, you should never seek her out without a proper chaperone. Nor should it be in the midst of the night. You should certainly never see the lady you are courting when she is in *dishabille*, wearing her nightdress and her dressing gown. You also should not see her hair unbound. Nor should you encourage her to address you in any less than a formal manner."

"That all sounds deadly boring to me," he told her. "It is fortunate indeed that I am not courting you."

Her chin tipped up. "I did not say you were. Nor would I accept your suit."

He frowned. "Why not?"

He should not ask, he knew. It mattered not. If Gill wanted to wed her, he would have her. Lord knew the coffers needed her funds. Besides, Ash was not the marrying sort. He liked living his life as he saw fit, unbound by vows. The very notion of chaining himself to one woman for the rest of his life, why, it made him...

Good God.

Strangely, the notion did not distress him as much as it once had. What the devil was the matter with him?

"You are a rake, my lord," she told him primly. "You think nothing of kissing ladies you have only recently met—"

"You are the only lady I have kissed since my arrival here," he interrupted, indignant in spite of himself.

"You are accustomed to ladies being wooed by your charm and your handsome face," she continued as if he had not spoken.

"My charm and my face are both impeccable," he added.

"And as I have already informed you, I have no desire to wed anyone," she finished. "I am beginning a foundling hospital of my own, and that is final."

A lovely woman like Miss Prudence Winter spending the rest of her life unmarried, her luscious body never touched, her innocence intact, was a sin in itself. She was a sensual creature. Her kisses had proven so.

"Do you truly wish to spend the rest of your life without ever knowing passion?" he demanded.

A voice inside him told him this was none of his concern. The guilt had never dissipated. It was still there, irritating as ever, and yet, a part of him seemed set upon overpowering it. Part of him railed against the notion of this woman becoming Gill's.

Because he wanted her to be his.

Bloody hell, there it was. The truth. The hideous, ridiculous truth.

He tamped it down, unable to face it. His brother had to come first. The estates had to come first. And for some reason, Gill had chosen Miss Prudence Winter. Hell, not for some reason—he knew damn well why. She was glorious.

But she had not answered him, either, and he found that curious. Curious and encouraging.

"Hmm, Miss Winter? Do you mean to never again kiss a man? To never know a lover's touch?" he asked, his voice going thick on the last query.

"You are impertinent," she charged. "What I choose to do, and the manner in which I spend my life, is none of your concern."

"But there is passion in you," he argued. "I felt it earlier, when we kissed. You do not seem like a lady who could happily live the rest of her life without knowing desire, just once."

He should stop, he knew. Stop talking. Stop goading her. Stop standing so damn close to her in the midst of the night. Stop inhaling the sweet scent of her.

But he could not.

"You do not even know me, my lord," she pointed out.

And once again, she was not wrong, Miss Prudence Winter. Everything about her was so alarmingly right.

"Mayhap I want to know you," he said, because he did. In all ways, confound it.

No matter how dreadfully shameful the acknowledgment felt.

And no matter how dreadfully wrong it was.

PRU SHOULD TAKE her brace of candles and return to the safety of her chamber.

Lingering in the darkness of the night, ensconced in the library and far away from the rest of the house guests, was not just foolish, but reckless as well. And yet, she could not seem to make her feet obey her. Instead, she remained mired as she was, rather like the anchor of a ship. Staring at Lord Ashley Rawdon, who had just announced he wanted to *know* her, of all things.

Ash, as he had suggested she call him. It was far too familiar—though, she supposed, no less familiar than kissing him had been. It was intimate in a way that was dangerous. She liked the sound of the shortened version of his name.

It suited the handsome devil before her.

"How should you presume to know me?" she asked him before she could stay the question. Before she could leave as she ought.

Had she not learned a blessed thing from *The Tale of Love*? Lingering in darkened libraries when rakes were beneath the same roof was a recipe for danger. The wickedest sort.

She shivered.

"Are you cold?" he queried instantly, taking note.

"Yes," she lied, because she did not want to admit the real reason for her reaction.

This unbearable attraction to him was not just unwanted—it was embarrassing. She was the eldest of all her sisters. She should have been the wisest. The most impervious to a fall.

"Come," he said, taking her hands in his.

His hands were warm and large, easily dwarfing hers. Capable too. She liked the way his skin felt against hers. And so, she allowed him to lead her to the far end of the cavernous library, to where the fire had been banked for the evening.

He walked backward, their fingers entwined, entering a portion of the chamber that seemed a whole different world compared to where she had left her brace of candles. This was a world, instead, of shadows and informality. Though he was very much a stranger to her, aside from their encounters at this house party, a sense of familiarity swept over Pru as he guided her across the room.

And not just familiarity, but comfort. Anticipation curled through her. Although she knew she should extricate herself from not just Lord Ashley's grasp but from this entire situation—indeed, this room—her body moved of its own accord. Her feet followed, step after step on the thick carpet as he led her deeper into darkness.

He maneuvered them past a desk and chairs, past some marble busts observing like silent sentinels over their midnight folly. How he navigated them so fluidly and effortlessly, she would never know. But suddenly, she found herself before the fire.

He released her hands at last and set to work upon it, adding a lone piece of wood and stoking the red-hot coals. Crackles echoed merrily through the space. He was still dressed in his breeches and shirt, but bereft of his coat, waistcoat, and cravat, lending the scene a whole new layer of intimacy.

She was all too aware she wore only her night rail and wrapper, slippers still on her feet to keep them from the chilled floors during her journey to the library. She had learned over the years that there was no more unpleasant sensation than a winter's floor in the depths of the night, for she was often plagued by restlessness and an inability to sleep.

Pru watched now as he bent and tended to the fire. How broad his back was, how long his torso, how strong his shoulders. When he lowered to his knees, she could not keep herself from admiring his haunches. Good heavens, his bottom was… Words and coherent thought deserted her. Was this why coats always kept a gentleman's full form hidden from view?

She could understand, ogling him now as she was—much to her shame—why. The man was positively indecent. His breeches hugged him lovingly, delineating every part of him. It was entrancing. She was helplessly in his thrall, forgetting all the reasons why she must not be here, forgetting the repercussions should anyone come upon them at this hour of the night.

He rolled back his shirtsleeves one by one, revealing long, strong forearms. She felt as if she had committed a sin merely by looking upon him in this low light, in this dangerous space where she could so easily fall into the forbidden.

She had to look away.

And she would, she promised herself. Just as soon as he finished prodding at the coals with the fire poker. Just as soon as he stood and turned to face her. She would stop looking. And she would also flee, as was wise.

But the fire was rising in the hearth, in an eerie echo of the heat rising inside her, filling her with a rich, striking warmth. Her face was hot. Still, she watched Lord Ashley working it, stoking the coals and wood to roaring flame.

Yet another eerie echo, it would seem, of what she felt within.

He replaced the poker and stood at last, apparently pleased with his work, turning to face her once more. Although he stood in shadows, her heart beat faster at the sight of him. He was so handsome. So disarmingly large and masculine. As a tall woman, not many men could make Pru feel dainty. And yet, this man did.

"Are you warmer now?" he asked softly.

She could not tell him the truth, that within, she was a fire to rival the flames crackling from the grate.

"Warmer," she repeated, feeling as if her tongue was heavy. Or perhaps her mind was sluggish. Stupefied by him. "Yes."

"Good," he said, staring at her, his gaze intent.

She wondered what he saw when he looked at her. The reflection awaiting her in the glass was always the same: hair the color of mud, without the sleek natural curl her sisters had inherited, eyes the same uninteresting hue, limbs too long, mouth too wide, hips too full.

All her sisters were beauties, perfectly feminine. But Pru was a head taller than Eugie, Christabella, Grace, and Bea. Horrid enough to be a reviled Winter whose family fortune had been founded in trade. But then to be a woman taller than most gentlemen...

But she must not linger over thoughts like that. Instead, she dismissed all such worries over her inadequacy. Instead, she felt as if she ought to remind him of how untoward this unguarded, unchaperoned moment between them was. She had long considered herself the most practical of all her sisters. Being alone with a rakehell like Lord Ashley Rawdon certainly suggested the opposite.

"I fear I must tell you another rule of proper courtship is that you should never remain alone with an unchaperoned lady in the library at midnight," she said. "Nor should you build her a fire and invite her to linger."

His lips twitched into a smile. "Ah, but the fire is for myself as much as it is for you, Miss Winter. It is deuced frigid in this cursed mausoleum, and my feet are cold. As for lingering, the choice is yours. I have not barred the door. You are free to go at any moment."

Of course she could not go. Not when she was enrobed in darkness with Lord Ashley.

Ash, whispered her impulsive heart.

"I am quite cold as well," she fibbed. "I shall remain long enough to warm myself before seeking my chamber."

"Come nearer, Miss Winter," he invited her.

She blinked. Surely he did not think she would be foolish enough to stand closer to him and tempt fate.

"I am perfectly fine here, thank you," she said coolly.

"Is standing near to a fire to warm one's self also against the rules of proper courtship?" he asked, raising a brow.

Drat him, even in the shadows, she could see enough of him to make a heavy sensation settle low in her belly. She refused to call it desire, though that was how *The Tale of Love* would refer to the restless urging, she was sure.

"It is against the rules when a gentleman and a lady are alone," she observed, aware of how prudish she sounded.

But then, her name *was* Prudence, was it not?

"Quite prudent of you," he said, almost as if he had read her thoughts. "Miss *Prudence* Winter."

Oh. Drat him twice over. That was a challenge if she had ever heard one, and there was no way the vexing man could have known it, but she had never met a challenge yet she could resist answering.

To that end, she stalked toward him, her defiance winning the battle. "I prefer to be called Pru," she found herself saying before she could think better of it.

She stopped alongside him. Together, they stood before the product of his effort, a merrily burning fire. Warmth suffused her, twofold. Lord Ashley Rawdon stood at her side, near enough to touch. So very alluring.

"Pru." He stretched out her name in that sweet, low baritone.

The effect of her name in his delicious voice settled between her thighs as a pulsing ache. In a wickedness she could not shake.

"Yes?" she asked, cautiously.

"It suits you."

The simple statement should not have affected her as it did. But she could not help but to turn toward him, studying his carved, aristocratic profile in the warm glow of the fire. Even from the side, and even enshrouded in mostly darkness, he was unfairly beautiful. That chin was so proud, his nose a thin, strong blade. His forehead and cheeks were high, but it was his mouth—oh, that sinful, wicked mouth—that truly called to her from any viewing vantage point.

"How so?" Her voice was strangled with an attempt to stifle the incipient burst of longing afflicting her.

His head turned, and he glanced down at her, the movement making their elbows brush. "Prudence means exercising caution. Showing restraint. But Pru is rather something between cautious restraint and recklessness, is it not? It is the abbreviated form. The form that can still be wild here and there, as it wishes. I fancy you may be wild when you wish, Pru. Am I wrong?"

She had never been wild.

At least, she did not think she had.

She had merely been herself, determined to find her way in the world. So many times, she found herself being the voice of caution and restraint for her sisters, and she could not deny it nettled. The role had never felt entirely right.

"I have never been wild." She paused, contemplating, before continuing. "I am the eldest of all my sisters, and in the absence of our mother, they look to me for maternal guidance."

"That is rather a hard weight to bear, is it not?" he prodded.

His astute assessment surprised her, reminding her not for the first time that there was far more to Lord Ashley Rawdon than a handsome face, fair form, and a rake's charm.

"It has been," she conceded. "But we are all of us similarly without our mother. And as I am the eldest, I naturally found myself in the role."

"Being the strongest of one's siblings is not always the easiest, is it?" His tone, like his question, was shrewd.

"I am not the strongest." She thought of Dev and the multitude of ways he had protected her and their sisters. "My brother is the one who has held us all together."

For Dev had. She and her siblings had been motherless for more of their lives than not. And their father had been a worthless scoundrel. A violent cad who was gone more often than he was at home. He had certainly not cared for Pru and her siblings. Instead, he had cared only for the amassing of his own fortune. In the end, he had not been able to take a ha'penny of it with him when he had passed from this life to the next.

"Perhaps not the strongest," Lord Ashley elaborated then, "but the one who is most capable of shouldering the burdens."

She wondered if he spoke from his own experience. His brother was the duke, but from what she had witnessed thus far over the course of the house party, Lord Ashley had spoken on behalf of himself and Coventry. It was plain that Coventry suffered from some sort of affliction which rendered him impossibly shy and cool. However, to hear Lord Ashley's wistful tone now confirmed her suspicions.

"Are you the brother most capable of bearing the weight of your familial burdens?" she asked him, although she knew she should not.

It was none of her affair whether or not Lord Ashley spent the remainder of his life acting as a proxy for his brother, the Duke of Coventry. She had no intention of binding herself to either one of them, as it happened. Why had she even posed such a question?

Lord Ashley swallowed, his attention still diverted toward the fire. The glow of the flames cast alternate flashes of brightness over his strong, handsome features. She studied him surreptitiously, unable to keep herself from watching.

He was that tempting.

"My brother suffered our father's temper far more brutally than I was ever forced to endure," Lord Ashley said, his tone vibrating with stark honesty.

His words resonated deep within her, for although her brother Dev had done his best to protect his siblings from their father's wrath, Father's cruelty was a bitter memory which would not soon be forgotten. Nor would the sting of his whip, lashing her until Dev had saved her one awful day.

"I am sorry, Lord Ashley," she said. "My father was not a kind man, and I know all too well the scars our pasts can leave upon us."

"Some on the heart, others on the flesh," he agreed. "Coventry endured more than any child ever should."

"That is one of the reasons I feel responsible for my sisters," she admitted. "I am the eldest, and we are motherless. Our father only cared to earn more coin, however he could."

It was the first time she had ever spoken those words aloud.

But saying them left her with such a feeling of peace. Of relief, almost. As if by the mere revelation, she had cut the ties of some of the chains binding her to the past.

"I understand," Lord Ashley said quietly, still staring into the fire in a most pensive fashion. "I feel the same. We are, all of us, bound in one fashion or another by our pasts, our blood, and our own senses of duty."

"Indeed we are," she agreed.

She wondered, then, if she had finally stumbled upon the true reason Lord Ashley was aiding Coventry in his search for a bride. Perhaps he did so out of obligation.

"Tell me something else about yourself, Pru," he invited before she could pursue the matter and pose another question.

"Are you asking on behalf of His Grace or do you ask for yourself?" she asked pointedly.

The delineation was clear to Pru: if he asked for the duke, she would say nothing. If he asked for himself, however…

"I ought to be asking on my brother's behalf," he conceded quietly, turning toward her once more. "But I am asking for myself."

The library suddenly felt as if it had been starved of air. Her heart was beating fast, and madly flitting butterflies were once more fluttering about in her belly. Their elbows brushed yet again as she shifted on her feet, trying to find her balance.

"What do you want to know about me?" The question left her, although she knew quite well she should not prolong this intimacy.

She could not seem to make herself leave, to force distance between them.

"Tell me something you have never told anyone else." His request, like the silky tone of his voice, was wicked.

Delicious.

"I will if you do," she countered, thinking she had bested him.

"I once dumped my father's unemptied chamber pot in his bed," Lord Ashley said, "I did it in the midst of the night whilst he was asleep, and I took great care to make certain nothing touched him. He woke to a foul mess, quite irate. He assumed it was Coventry who had done it, and my brother accepted his punishment without ever mentioning I was the guilty one."

She had not expected a confession from him at all. But this one—it was shocking, slightly humorous, and rather sad, all at once. It also told her a great deal about Lord Ashley Rawdon, she thought.

"Is that why you feel so indebted to your brother?" she dared.

"One of the reasons, perhaps," he allowed. "One of many. But that is neither here nor there. I have revealed my something I have never told anyone else to you. You must now tell me one of yours."

She thought for a moment.

There was the time she had poured salt into Grace's pillow. The time she had hidden a wedge of cheese beneath Christabella's bed in the heart of summer. The day she had secreted a toad in Eugie's chamber pot...

But, no. She did not wish to confess her childish pranks. They were all horridly embarrassing.

"Pru," Lord Ashley urged, "I have yet to hear a word from your pretty lips. Out with it."

He thought her lips were pretty?

Heavens, how was she to form coherent thought after such a revelation?

She heaved a sigh and thought some more. One came to mind, an old source of great shame. "I stole a ribbon once."

"A ribbon," he repeated, disappointment tingeing his voice. "I am afraid you will have to do better than that, Pru."

"That is a shocking and horrifying secret I have never told another," she argued. "I am horridly ashamed of my behavior to this day."

"A ribbon," he said again.

"Yes," she countered, "a ribbon. I was at a milliner's, ordering new hats with my sisters, and we were being shown such expensive accents, such glorious styles. It was my brother's first attempt at making us respectable. One of the ribbons was the most beautiful shade of blue I had ever seen."

Rather like Lord Ashley's eyes.

She banished the thought and continued.

"It was a special, new dye. Quite rare and expensive, the milliner informed us. The finest silk ribbon. I decided I needed to have it," she recalled grimly. "And I stuffed it into my reticule when no one was looking."

The moment she had committed the sin, she had been horrified by what she had done. And yet, she had been too terrified to remove the ribbon. She had been terribly young at the time, dreadfully foolish also. To this day, she could not comprehend what impulse had made her stuff the ribbon inside her reticule. To take it when she could have paid for it a thousand times over.

"You are a thief, Pru," he said.

"Yes," she agreed, wresting her gaze from his handsome profile and turning it instead into the flames. "I am."

"Do you have it still?" he asked, his tone considering.

"Do I have what?" she asked, flustered. From the elbow rubbing and the darkness and his beauty and the sharing of secrets.

One of her most shameful.

Truly, she had been hoping to never tell another soul about her ignominy, but something about sharing it with Lord Ashley felt oddly as if it lifted a weight from her shoulders.

"The ribbon," he elaborated. "Do you still have the stolen ribbon? I must confess, I do like to think of perfectly prudent Pru being most imprudent, even if only once. Was it just the once, or were there other occasions?"

"It was just the once," she said. "I have never stolen a thing in my life since that day. I still have no notion of what came over me."

"Rebelliousness." The lone, simple word in his deep baritone made a trill shoot straight through her. "You were tired of always doing what was proper, what was expected of you."

She glanced back toward him, and this time, he had turned to give her his full attention as well. The effect was enough to make her breath catch. Part of her longed to acknowledge he was right. Part of her feared what it meant, this dangerous rakehell, knowing her so well.

Better than she knew herself.

"It was foolishness," she corrected, doing her best to remind herself of all the reasons why she could not linger here with him.

Not for another second longer.

For if she did, the same impulse that had led her to steal

that ribbon so long ago was bound to return and overcome her all over again.

"Pru," he said, his voice a low rasp.

Pure seduction. He reached for her.

She stepped away, hugging herself. "I must go, my lord. Thank you for warming me by the fire, and for the pleasant conversation. But I dare not tarry here any longer."

Without awaiting his response, she turned away and fled. Hurried across the library and into the empty corridor. She did not stop her flight until she had reached the safety of her chamber. As the door clicked closed behind her and she heaved a sigh of relief, it occurred to her that she had neglected to choose a book, as had been her initial intention.

It had not been the first time Lord Ashley Rawdon had made her forget what she was supposed to do. She had a rather damning feeling that it would not be the last, either.

Chapter Five

*M*ISS PRUDENCE WINTER was a thief.

Ash was still thinking about the revelation she had made the next afternoon whilst he was taking a brisk walk in the Abingdon Hall maze with Gill. They had eschewed the afternoon's frivolity in favor of time away from the rest of the company, where they could speak freely. Even if it was bloody cold out this afternoon.

Her secret had not been the first indication Pru did not always do what was proper.

She had kissed him, after all. Damnation, how she had kissed him. It had been the kiss which had ruined him. But perhaps the predicament in which he now found himself was not the fault of the kiss, but rather of the lady herself.

Pru.

Tall, glorious, lush-lipped Pru of the twin dimples, whose long legs he could not stop imagining wrapped around his waist as he sank his cock deep inside her tight, wet heat.

Fucking hell. He had to banish all such thoughts immediately. Forever.

"Have you had occasion to speak with her?" he prodded his brother at last, goaded into action by his inner guilt and inner frustration both.

"Miss Winter?" Gill asked.

"Of course," he gritted. "Who else?"

Gill nodded. "I have spoken with her."

When? Some possessive urge inside him made him clench his fists at his sides. He had not seen Gill anywhere near Pru this morning. Not at breakfast. Nor later…

But then he forced himself to recall that this was the natural progression of things. Just like a babe was born, grew older, and eventually withered away, he would have to accept these devilish yearnings for Miss Prudence Winter would necessarily dissipate. When she was the Duchess of Coventry, in his brother's arms and his brother's bed, he would have no choice but to forget her.

Why did the notion make him feel as if he needed to cast up his accounts into the nearest hedge?

"And what is your opinion of her?" he forced himself to ask next.

"She is…" his brother's words trailed off.

"She is?" he prodded, vexed. He had no wish to wait to hear his brother wax on about all Pru's lovely attributes. For he saw them all himself, and he coveted them.

He coveted *her.*

"She is loquacious," Gill pronounced grimly. "Thinks she can aid me. I have told her I do not require her assistance, yet she will not accept my refusal."

This was news.

"What does she think she can help you with?" he asked, as curious as he was irritated by the thought of Pru assisting his brother with anything.

"Courting," Gill said, ever terse.

"What the devil?" Ash stopped, facing his brother as if they were two fighters in Grey's boxing salon. He certainly felt pugnacious in that moment. "That sounds precisely like the aid she offered me. What did you tell her?"

"No," his brother said, but it was either the frigid air or

embarrassment that had painted Gill's slashing cheekbones bright red. And it sounded like a falsehood.

It occurred to him that his brother had just admitted to engaging in a conversation with a female. With Pru, specifically.

"You have been speaking with her," he added.

It was deuced unlike Gill to speak to ladies at all.

Gill's gaze flicked away, inspecting something over Ash's shoulder as if it held him in its thrall. "A bit."

Curse it, Ash was equally torn between being thrilled his brother had actually deigned to speak to the fairer sex and mind-numbingly jealous over the fact that it was Pru who had inspired him to break free of the anxiety that gripped him in social situations. Why did it have to be Pru? Why could it not have been someone else? There were ladies aplenty at this damned house party.

But then he asked himself why it should matter.

He had no desire to wed himself, and he could not dally with unwed ladies. Nor with Pru, the woman his brother had chosen. The very same woman who stirred him in a way no other woman had.

Ever.

A violent burst of winter wind hit them, bringing with it a flutter of powdery snow. It hit Ash in the face in a storm of icy pinpricks, jolting him from his musings. Gill was still staring into the distance, his expression unreadable.

He unclenched his fists. If Gill married Pru, Ash would have to banish the terrible attraction he felt for her. "You feel comfortable with her, then," he observed, unable to keep the bitterness from his voice.

Gill's gaze jerked back to Ash's, a frown furrowing his brow beneath his hat. "I…she confounds me. But yes, there is something about her that also puts me at ease, strange as it sounds."

Perhaps that was one of Pru's gifts.

Ash could not shake the grimness within him. It was a devil of a predicament to find one's self in. He ought to be pleased. Relieved, even. He had attended this blasted house party to help his brother find a wife. Not to lust after Gill's choice of bride himself.

"That is excellent," he forced himself to say. "When she is your duchess, you may find it easier to engage in the social whirl if she is at your side."

And Ash himself would stay far, far away.

"When she is my duchess?" Gill's frown deepened.

"Yes," Ash gritted. "You are still settled upon marrying Miss Prudence Winter, are you not?"

His brother's frown cleared. "Er, yes, of course I am. I was not speaking of Miss Prudence Winter, however, but of her sister, Miss Christabella."

Relief he had no right to feel washed over Ash. Cleansing him. He felt like a new man. This was trouble. And speaking of trouble…

"You have been talking to the flame-haired sister?" he asked his brother. "The one who is always chattering and wearing bright-colored dresses?"

"That one." Gill's jaw tensed. "Loquacious, as I said. Red-haired. Does not take no for an answer."

Thank Christ. But still, of all the Winter sisters, the wild one seemed the least likely candidate to set his brother at ease and inspire such an unprecedented response.

"I thought you were speaking of Miss Prudence," he admitted. "Have you spoken to her yet?"

"Directly?" Gill's frown returned. "No."

"Ah," he said, infinitely pleased by the revelation.

"Have *you* been speaking with her?" his brother prodded,

curiosity in his tone.

Ash cleared his throat, the guilt returning in full force. "A small amount. Here and there. Scarcely at all, really."

"Miss Prudence wants to assist you with courting?" Gill asked.

Damn.

"She offered me aid in observing the proprieties when courting ladies," he admitted. "Yes."

His brother laughed. "Does she not know you do not give a damn about propriety?"

That much was true. He did not give a damn about it.

He did, however give a damn about Pru. Far, far too much of a damn. And any excuse to be near to her or to have more of her time was one he would seize with both greedy hands. Apparently, his mouth, too.

"Perhaps she thinks she is performing a service for her fellow sex," he evaded lightly. "It matters not, for I only agreed so that I might get a bit more acquainted with her and determine whether or not the two of you would suit."

"Selfless of you, brother," Gill quipped. "You have my thanks."

But there was a goading edge in his brother's tone that made Ash wonder if there was something else at work, some underlying emotion. Surely he did not suspect Ash of being improper with Pru?

"I have not compromised her, if that is what you are implying," he ground out, the river of guilt threatening to drown him from within lending a sharpness to his voice.

Gill's brow raised. "I did come upon the two of you in the salon. Alone. Miss Winter seemed rather flushed."

The guilt turned into an ocean.

But Ash was saved from having to respond by the timely arrival of a snowball. The snowball landed in the center of

Gill's chest, broke upon impact, and rained to their feet in its own miniature snowstorm. The expression of shock on his brother's face could not be duplicated.

"Oh dear," said a feminine voice. "Do forgive me, Your Grace. I fear my aim was misplaced."

He turned to find Miss Prudence and Miss Christabella Winter several paces away. The latter was the guilty party, her gloved hands coated with a telltale layer of snow.

THE ASTONISHED EXPRESSIONS on both the Duke of Coventry's and Lord Ashley's handsome countenances were enough to make a burst of laughter startle from Pru. She had to admit that sometimes Christabella's playful nature took her by surprise. Neither of them had expected to cross paths with the duke and his brother when they had set out on their walk in the extensive holly mazes of Abingdon Hall.

They had escaped from the afternoon's drawing room entertainments to have a sisterly chat—Pru's idea, for Christabella had still yet to reveal the extent of what wickedness she had been engaged in with the Duke of Coventry the other night. It had been an aberration, Christabella had reassured her, with no chance of it being repeated.

But Pru knew her sister, and she remained unconvinced. Precisely why Christabella was enamored with Coventry, however, Pru could still not determine. Whilst the duke was undeniably handsome, Christabella made no secret of her longing to snare a rake for herself. There was nothing at all rakish about the shy, icy duke.

Pru had been prodding Christabella to reveal more details when they rounded the corner of the maze and discovered they were not alone. Although Lord Ashley's back had been facing them, Pru would recognize his tall, lean form anywhere. Even in a hat and greatcoat, there was no hiding the broadness of his shoulders. He was wearing boots and perfectly fitted breeches, and he was so handsome she had to suppress a sigh.

And tamp down her reaction to him.

Forget about the way he had looked in the firelight.

Forget about how the merest grazing of his elbow against hers made her melt.

Christabella had saved her by scooping up a handful of snow from her feet and packing it between her gloved hands.

"Watch this," she had announced with a wicked grin and a gleam in her eyes.

And then, she had proceeded to catapult a snowball at a duke.

The remnants of her missile were still stuck to Coventry's chest as he and Lord Ashley gawked at them.

"Forgive my sister, Your Grace," Pru felt compelled to call out. "She did not intend to hit you with the snowball. Are you injured?"

The duke's expression looked as if it had been chiseled in stone.

"Actually, I did mean to hit you," Christabella added, unrepentant. "But I was aiming for your hat."

"That was a childish prank, madam," the duke said, his baritone low and gravelly.

That his voice sounded so strange to Pru's ears was a testament to how little Coventry spoke. He did not appear entertained by Christabella's sally or her daring, and Pru could hardly blame him. Who would possibly wish to be hit with a snowball?

"Forgive me, Your Grace." Christabella grinned. "As you know, I am beset by an inability to behave."

Coventry made a strangled sound, half-animalistic growl, half-disapproval. But then he did the strangest thing. He sank to his haunches, gathering up some snow in several swift motions. Then he lobbed his snowball in their direction.

The snowball hit Christabella's bonnet and broke, sending snow raining down into her face.

"Oh, you bounder!" Christabella exclaimed, but there was no outrage in her voice, only laughter. "That was one of my best hats!"

Coventry grinned back at her. "I was merely showing you an example of excellent aim, Miss Winter."

"That is the outside of enough," Christabella announced. "I declare this a war. Pru, start making snowballs."

Pru's gaze swung to her sister. "What can you be think-ing? We cannot begin throwing snowballs at gentlemen. It simply is not done. Why, Dev would have our hides if he knew we were out here engaging in such hoydenish behavior, and I must insist you—"

A snowball hit her own bonnet then, interrupting her chastisement. She blinked and coughed as a snow cloud enveloped her face. Christabella's tinkling laughter mocked her. She turned back to Lord Ashley and the duke, all the outrage inside her withering when she caught sight of the boyish grin on Lord Ashley's lips.

"Did you dare to throw a snowball at me, Lord Ashley?" she demanded.

"Yes, I did," he admitted without a hint of shame. If anything, his tone—like his expression—was smug. "Your sister announced this is war, after all. We must defend ourselves."

Oh, it was war indeed.

She bent low, and packed her own ball of snow, which she hurtled in his direction. It landed at his feet, breaking on his boots.

"Drat," she muttered.

"Put more force into it," Christabella counseled as snow-balls began raining around them.

"Is that the best you can do, ladies?" taunted Lord Ashley.

"Let's get them," Pru told her sister grimly, forgetting all about being ladylike.

She and Christabella launched into battle, scooping up heaps of snow, molding it into balls, and hurling them at their opponents as they laughingly dodged the ammunition being thrown at them in return. A snowball hit her on the shoulder, sending a cloud of snow into her face. Another hit the hem of her gown. Christabella was hit in the arm.

Pru could not recall when she had laughed so hard. She giggled until her lungs and sides ached. And though her fingers were icy beneath her gloves, she could not seem to stop. There was something undeniably thrilling about engaging in such childish silliness.

Suddenly, Coventry and Lord Ashley took off running, disappearing around the bend in the maze.

"Get them!" Christabella cried, much like a general leading an infantry charge.

Pru gathered her gown in her snow-covered fists and chased after her sister in the wake of the lords they had sent running. She could not stop laughing, but as they rounded the bend, she realized the maze grew more intricate, branching off in two separate directions.

Neither Coventry nor Lord Ashley were anywhere to be found, though there were footprints tracked through the snow on both paths. Breathless, about to turn into an icicle herself and yet not giving a care, she turned to her sister.

"Which way do you think they went?"

"You go to the right," Christabella ordered. "I will go to

the left."

Pru's feet were carrying her before her mind could argue she would be better off to remain put. Or to go back inside and thaw by a roaring fire. Some of Christabella's wildness must have wormed its way into Pru, for she was giggling, racing through the snow as if she had not a care in all the world.

Until she turned a corner and smacked directly into a wall.

She lost her balance and would have fallen backward, landing on her rump, were it not for the strong hands that shot out to catch her waist, hauling her back into the wall. Which, as it turned out, was not a wall at all. But rather, a chest.

A broad, muscled, delicious chest.

Her head tipped back, and she was even more breathless than she had been before as bright-blue eyes burned into hers.

"Lord Ashley," she managed to say.

"Caught you," he growled, and there was such satisfaction in his voice, she could not help but to feel it.

Everywhere.

Her hands went to his shoulders. It was all so effortless. So natural.

So right.

Neither the duke nor Christabella were in sight. Lord Ashley was all she saw. His smiling lips, his gleaming eyes, the snow on his hat from one of the snowballs she had landed, his handsome face. A new ache pulsed to life within her, and she could not squelch the desire to feel his lips on hers.

"You may release me now," she said, irritated with herself at how winded she sounded.

As if she had run a lap around the sprawling Abingdon House instead of a mere few feet in the gardens. He had such a devastating effect upon her. But then, she reminded herself, surely she was not the only one so afflicted by Lord Ashley Rawdon.

Because otherwise, he would not be a notorious rake.

"I could release you," he murmured, his gaze settling on her lips. "Or I could keep you just where you are. And that seems far more pleasing to me at the moment, Pru, I must confess."

It did to her as well, but that was the problem. She liked this man too much. And liking him would lead her only down the wrong garden path. The irony was not lost on her.

"You *should* release me," she managed to say thickly.

Her mind was waging war with the rest of her. Because her mind knew everything about lingering here in the maze with Lord Ashley, out of sight of her sister and the duke, was dangerous. It was like an invitation to sin.

Much like the man himself.

"I should," he agreed, making no move to do so, the scoundrel. "But much like you were tempted by that ribbon, I am tempted to steal what should not be mine."

She swallowed hard. "I am not for sale."

"Nor are you for me," he said softly, his stare intense upon hers. "Still, I cannot seem to resist you, Pru. I should not want to kiss you again, either. But I do."

His admission sent a wave of heat crashing over her from the inside out, chasing the cold of the snow and the frigid air. Chasing everything but the man before her, the tantalizing promise of his lips on hers once again. Had she ever wanted anything more?

If she had, she could not recall it.

"That is against the rules of proper courting," she whispered.

But she made no move to extricate herself from his embrace either. Because she liked being precisely where she was. She liked the way his tall, lean body fitted against hers. The way he stood a head above, the way he looked down at her as if she were something he desperately longed to devour.

This man was bad, and she liked it.

"I am beginning to suspect that proper courting is a deadly bore," Lord Ashley said then, tipping his head toward hers. "Just as I always thought it was. There are far more interesting ways to spend one's time, Pru."

"Oh?" She wetted her lips.

They were icy and yet aflame. She was cold and yet hot. She did not want him and yet she did. It was such a confusing dichotomy, rolling through her. Overpowering her in a way she had never before experienced. Rather like an unexpected storm.

"Oh, yes," he said, that wicked mouth of his twitching into a scoundrel's grin of sensual promise.

But before he could kiss her as she so desperately longed for him to do, the sound of Christabella's and Coventry's laughter reached them, along with the shuffle of their feet through the snow. It was a warning both she and Lord Ashley heeded.

They sprang apart just as their siblings appeared, snow-covered and giggling.

"That was the best snowball fight I have ever had," Christabella declared.

"It was the only one I have ever had," Coventry muttered, looking suddenly bemused.

Pru swept toward her sister. "Amusing diversion though it was, it would not do for either of us to linger here in the cold."

Linking her arm through her sister's before anyone could protest, Pru practically hauled her from the maze.

Chapter Six

$\mathcal{E}$ARLY THE NEXT morning, Ash braved the stinging
December chill to go riding with Gill and Viscount
Aylesford. They made a grim trio, guiding their mounts over
the snow-covered field in mutual silence. His brother was
always quiet. Aylesford seemed to be vexed over something,
his countenance as harsh as a summer thundercloud.

For his part, Ash was struggling to make sense of his
problem.

The problem which was growing exponentially larger by
the day, by the hour, by the bloody minute. The problem was
not just the ordinary variety any longer. It was all-consuming,
taking over Ash's every thought like an invading army
commanded to wage war. The problem was getting stronger
and more unavoidable.

It was also damned stupid.

As the product of a loveless union between a heartless
scoundrel and a frivolous woman who had paid more
attention to her endless string of lovers than she ever had to
her sons, Ash had vowed to never seek out the infernal
institution of matrimony. As the spare, he had no need to,
after all. He had the luxury of choosing his bed partners, of
avoiding the parson's mousetrap, of never needing to wed at
all.

Instead, he was free to spend his days in pursuit of diversion and anything in skirts. His life was his own. He was happy and complete with having no greater responsibility than finding his next bed partner. The small annual income he received—which had been out of his wastrel sire's reach, thankfully—was enough. He needed nothing more.

Until he had first clashed wits with Pru.

And then, all the ways he had squandered his days previously—drinking, gaming, racing horses, and devoting himself to all manner of gentlemanly sport—no longer appealed. All those things which had once sustained him now felt remarkably hollow. Unsatisfying, even.

It was a hell of a realization.

A terrifying one, in fact. Bloody confusing as well. Particularly since the lady around which his problem revolved was the same lady he was meant to be assisting his brother in wooing. He was wooing her, indeed.

But he was wooing her for himself.

"Fucking legend," Aylesford muttered suddenly, cutting through the mutual silence and Ash's miserable thoughts both.

Ash's gaze swung to the viscount, certain he had misheard. "What was that, Aylesford? Did you just say *fucking legend*?"

"He did," Gill said.

A vengeful gust of icy winter's wind blasted them, nearly making off with Aylesford's hat. He clamped a hand down on the brim, holding on to the reins with the other.

"I said *you* are a fucking legend," he told Ash, unblinking.

Ash did not know precisely what Aylesford meant by his quip. He did not know the viscount terribly well beyond the bounds of this house party, though they did travel in the same circles. Aylesford himself was a notorious rakehell, so for all Ash knew, it was perfectly ordinary for him to congratulate another gentleman upon his bedchamber conquests.

If that was indeed what Aylesford was implying.

"Ah, but am I a *fucking* legend or a fucking *legend*?" he returned wryly, grinning. "That is the question."

"Is it true that you tupped an opera singer, an actress, and a nun all at once?" Aylesford asked, giving voice to the old rumor that had been plaguing Ash for years.

In his youth, he had considered the rumor a badge of honor. Now, it rather felt like a hollow victory. He had been a scandalous rakehell when he had been a stripling, but he had tamed his wilder ways in recent years. Some of the memories were fonder than others…

"Not true at all," he explained, desperate for any dialogue so long as it struck thoughts of Pru from his mind. "The actress in question had been playing the role of a nun in her latest play. The opera singer did not resemble a nun in the slightest."

"Ash," chided Coventry. "We discussed this."

Yes, of course they had. Gill did not want Ash's reputation—and his well-known sins—to have a negative impact upon his brother's ability to gain a bride. Ironically enough, Gill had far more to worry about in the present than he had in the past.

Much to Ash's everlasting shame.

"Ah, how could I forget?" Ash could not resist casting a derisive glance toward his brother. "I am to hide my past lest it muddy the waters for brother dearest as he attempts to find himself a bride. Familial obligations and all that rot."

"Bugbears," Gill told him. "I am yours. You are mine."

"Bugbears indeed," Aylesford grumbled.

A man such as he undoubtedly had more than a few of his own.

"Poor Gill has no choice but to wed because he inherited," he told the viscount, feeling the need to offer explanation on behalf of his brother, as he so oft did. "Our father was a reckless wastrel. Could not be trusted with a ha'penny. Now Gill gets to pay the price. However, he is not particularly known for his ability to woo the fairer sex."

"You are his rearguard, as it were," Aylesford suggested.

Yes, much to his irritation. Because all he wanted to do was romance his brother's choice of bride himself, *curse it*. But he could not say this aloud.

"Precisely," he said instead. "Brilliant, Aylesford. I am my brother's romantic rearguard. I save his army from impending doom. Particularly, Miss Christabella Winter."

It had not escaped Ash's notice that his brother was doing rather a lot of speaking to and about the wrong Miss Winter. The wild one with the red hair who had begun the entire snowball affair.

"Miss Winter is assisting me," Gill bit out, glaring at him.

Though Ash had attempted to speak with his brother yesterday following the impromptu snowball fight they had shared with Pru and Miss Christabella in the gardens, they had forever been interrupted by fellow guests. And then, Gill had gone to bed early whilst Ash had stayed awake, downing brandy and his guilt all at once. He rather suspected now that Gill had been avoiding him.

Because as much as Ash did not want Gill to marry Pru, he was also horrified at the prospect of his brother taking on such a troublesome baggage as Miss Christabella Winter as his duchess. Moreover, how could anyone—given the choice between the two sisters—not see how eminently more alluring Pru was?

"She is the wrong Miss Winter," he snapped at Gill. "You said you wish to marry Miss Prudence, did you not? She is the eldest and the loveliest of all the Winter sisters. Miss Christabella cannot compare. If you would simply cease spending all your time being distracted by the hellion and instead woo the woman you are meant to wed, your chance of success would increase immeasurably. Before someone else takes your place."

Before I take your place, he meant to say.

The words were there, waiting on his tongue.

Nearly suspended in the chilly air.

And yet, he could not speak them. Did not dare, for what it would mean, not only to his relationship with his brother, but also to himself. He still could not fathom how or why he could want a woman as much as his traitorous body wanted Pru's. He did not just lust after her; rather, he wanted to possess her. He wanted to make her his and only his, to keep her forever…

"Here now," Aylesford intervened. "I would argue Miss Grace is the loveliest of all the Winters by far. With her auburn hair and flashing green eyes, not to mention her perfect pink lips…"

Was the man mad? Or was he merely hopelessly in Miss Grace Winter's thrall? They were engaged to be wed, after all, but Ash had rather assumed it was a marriage of convenience. Now, he could not help but to wonder.

Aylesford trailed off before clearing his throat, his cheeks darkening to an undeniably embarrassed hue of scarlet that had nothing to do with the violent December wind and everything to do with whatever thoughts were roiling in the man's mind.

"In love, are you, Aylesford?" Ash could not resist taunting, his lips twitching.

What a relief it was to think upon the suffering of others instead of his own torment for the nonce.

"Love?" the viscount repeated, scoffing. "Such an emotion is better suited to fools and naïve women who sigh over silly novels filled with drivel. Do you not think?"

"I believe love is possible," Gill said.

What the bloody, fucking hell? Since when had his brother ever believed in love? They had both been born into the same web of misery. Unless...*by God*, he refused to believe it. Nay, surely not. And still, once the notion entered his mind, it refused to go away until he did something.

"With Pru?" Ash demanded before he could think better of the query.

"Pru?" his brother repeated, raising a mocking brow at him.

Damn it all, he was showing his hand like a poor player at cards. And making a fool of himself too. He had to do something—anything—to prove he was as unmoved by Pru as ever.

"*Miss Prudence Winter*," he amended, making a great show of flicking a speck of imaginary lint from the sleeve of his greatcoat as he held the reins in a loose grasp with his left hand. "You know to whom I refer."

"I did not question whom but rather your familiarity," Gill said pointedly.

Ash could have said the same thing to his brother about Miss Christabella Winter. But in that moment, he was filled with such a rare mixture of anger, guilt, and irritation—at himself, at Gill—that his only recourse was escape. He was riding a horse, and there was an open expanse ahead of him, *curse it*.

"Go to the devil," he told Gill.

With that, he spurred his mount into a gallop, putting as much distance as he could between himself, his brother, and the mountain of guilt that wanted to bury him whole.

❄

PRU WAS NOT hiding, she told herself as she settled into the false ruins of Abingdon Hall. There were few drawing room entertainments today as most of the company was diverting themselves with sleigh rides in the snow. She had taken the opportunity to seize some time to herself, away from everyone.

Away from one deliciously handsome rake in particular.

Lord Ashley Rawdon was a temptation she was finding it increasingly difficult to resist. And resist him she must, for her future depended upon it. She had engaged in a stern talk with herself yesterday evening, following the snowball fight and their almost-kiss.

There was nothing she wanted more than to begin her own foundling hospital. Not only did she love children, but she knew all too keenly the plight of those who were born to unwed mothers, or to families who were unable to feed them, or even to families who ill-used and ill-treated them.

And spending time alone with a rake, putting her reputation in danger, meant she was also putting the prospect of her own foundling house in peril. If she were caught engaging in improper behavior with Lord Ashley, she would be forced to marry him—if he would even come up to scratch and make an offer for her, that was. The harsh truth she needed to face was that men like Lord Ashley toyed with women for sport, but they did not settle down and allow themselves to be caught in the parson's mousetrap. If they did, they invariably made their wives miserable as they carried on with their licentiousness.

Pru was pragmatic. She had heard far too many tales of woe. She was not a romantic like Christabella, foolishly believing she would be the one to turn a rake's head and lead him to change his wicked ways. She understood what Lord Ashley was, and she understood what she was.

There was no world that existed in which they would find

a shared path.

He was dallying with her, there was no doubt about it. And probably because he was bored. If she kept her distance from him, she had told herself, he would find someone else at the house party to dally with instead. Someone far more amenable to the chase.

Oh, who was she fooling? She was amenable to the chase. She wanted his attention, his stare, his mouth on hers, his arms banding around her. She wanted his tall, lean warmth melting into hers.

And that was the biggest problem of all.

Heaving a sigh, Pru threw herself into a settee positioned near the happily crackling fire lit in the grate. The beauty of the false ruins was lost upon her, though it was striking from the approach. Surrounded by snow and pines, the outbuilding had been fashioned to look as if it were a Greek ruin from the outside. On the inside, however, was a charming series of rooms, connected by a great hall, each comfortably furnished and with a fire to provide warmth whilst the guests were in residence.

Ordinarily, it was just the sort of place she would love to spend a few hours of solitude. But today, she was feeling restless and grim. Foolish and weary. The strange sensation that plagued her whenever she was in Lord Ashley's presence had not gone away yesterday as it had on previous occasions. Instead, it had lingered. By the time she had gone to bed last night, it had worsened.

She knew what it was, thanks to *The Tale of Love*.

Desire.

She wanted Lord Ashley. Wanted to be tempted by him, taken by him, kissed and touched and ruined by him.

And for those reasons and many more, she was hiding. Again?

Hiding where she was certain no one would look. Traveling to the false ruin required a fifteen-minute walk down a snow-laden path. She had dressed warmly for the occasion, donning her sturdiest boots, a fur muffler, a coat, and a hat and scarf. But by the time she had reached the ruins, she had been chilled to the bone. Thank heavens for the fire. Servants would arrive to tend to it on the hour, but until then, she was happily, blissfully, alone.

Also, determined to distract her mind from all improper thoughts.

She would banish Lord Ashley Rawdon from her mind, from her life, from her stupid, restless yearnings. Pru opened the book she had brought along to aid in her diversion. As it happened, it was a volume of *The Tale of Love* she had yet to read, because another wicked rake—Viscount Aylesford—was in possession of the last volume she'd been reading after she had loaned it to her sister Grace.

But that was another story all its own, and she did not dare to allow her mind to linger on rakehells and scoundrels, because if she did, it would inevitably lead back to He Whom She Refused to Name.

Instead, she flipped through her book, settling upon the chapter where she had last left off. This chapter was written in the epistolary form, one letter from a lady to her friend, describing all the joy she had found from a gentleman she had met in London.

The joy was licentious, of course. The gentleman in question was no gentleman at all. The descriptions of what he had done to the lady were vivid and naughty. And Pru wanted to know more.

But just as she began devouring the words on the page, the door to the chamber clicked open. She glanced up, expecting a servant who had come to tend the fire. But she found, instead, the only man she was seeking to avoid.

"Lord Ashley," she said, unable to keep the dismay from her voice as she jumped from the settee and dropped into a curtsy, careful to hide her book from his view.

He bowed, flashing her a wry grin. "Do not sound so pleased to see me, or you shall make me grow hopelessly vain, Pru."

She really had to stop him from being so familiar with her, she thought. But the trouble was, she liked hearing her name in his husky voice.

"It is improper for you to be here," she explained, needlessly. Of course, he already knew that. "Did you follow me?"

She was expecting him to deny it.

Instead, he met her gaze frankly. "Yes."

Oh, the wicked man. How was she to resist him now? He was closing the door at his back, and then his long strides ate up the distance between them. He was still wearing his greatcoat, with a dusting of flurries on the shoulders. He removed his hat when he stood before her. It, too, was crusted with a fine sheen of snow.

His blue eyes were mesmerizing as they met hers. No matter how much she steeled herself against his magnetic charm and the inevitable effect he had upon her, there was no way to remain impervious. Not when he towered over her, his lips so full and perfect, his cheekbones strong slashes, his jaw angular, his chin proud. Why did he have to be so dratted irresistible?

The scent of his cologne, warm and musky and decadent, hit her, along with the fresh scent of the outdoors. She wanted to throw herself into his arms. But she did not. Instead, he stared at her, his gaze seeming to touch her like a caress. Devouring her, it was true.

It was her turn to speak, she realized then.

"Why did you follow me?" she asked, attempting to summon her outrage.

His lips quirked. "For the usual reason, I expect. I wanted to speak with you alone."

"Being alone together is foolhardy," she said, irritated with herself.

Her heart was beating too fast. The ache that had never stopped since their near kiss yesterday throbbed with urgency. Despite her good intentions, she was looking at him and imagining all the forbidden acts she had read about in *The Tale of Love*.

He peeled off his gloves and tossed them, along with his hat, to the settee's cushion, his air indolent. As if he had all the time in the world. And not a care.

"Is it against the rules of proper courting?" he asked unrepentantly, his gaze fixed upon hers as he shrugged his greatcoat from his deliciously broad shoulders. "I confess, I do not know. A mutual acquaintance of ours was supposed to teach me, and she has been neglecting her duties."

Of course she had been neglecting their silly wager. How was she meant to keep it up when all she wanted to do was kiss him and throw all caution out the window whenever she was in his presence?

She tipped up her chin, clinging to defiance, her only defense against him. "Perhaps I have decided to forego our wager. After all, you never had any intention of visiting my foundling hospital."

He tossed his coat upon the settee, and it landed atop the discarded hat. Still, he did not wrest his eyes from her. "You may be surprised what I would do on your behalf, Pru. Hell, I think I would even surprise myself."

How unfair it was for him to say such a thing to her.

He was close enough to touch.

And she wanted to touch him.

"Stop," she commanded him.

"Stop what?" He took a step closer, crowding her with his big body.

Tempting her, too.

"Stop saying things you do not mean," she forced herself to say. "Stop using your flattery and silver tongue upon me. I know this is a game to you, Lord Ashley, but it is not a game to me. This is my life you are toying with."

Her voice broke on the last word, and she hated herself for that weakness. For the way he affected her. For the ability he alone possessed to make her so vulnerable. Vulnerable in a way she had imagined she was not capable of being, for she was the eldest Winter sister. The wisest. The most reasonable. The most pragmatic and calm.

The sister least likely to cause a scandal.

And yet, here she stood, oh-so-tempted to launch herself into this beautiful scoundrel's arms.

He reached out. Just his forefinger. The fleshy pad of it caressed her chin. Her heart leapt. The aching need for him turned into a steady throb, beginning at her core and radiating outward, suffusing her in a heavy warmth.

"I have never uttered a word to you that I did not mean, Pru," he said then, softly. "There is no flattery for you. There is only truth. I have never been drawn to another as I am drawn to you."

She forgot how to breathe.

At least, that was how it seemed as his words settled over her.

"My lord," she protested.

He traced a path up her chin, pressing his finger against her lips, silencing her. "Ash."

She closed her eyes, trying to find her strength. But her

attraction for him was so potent, it was overwhelming. She refused to say his name. Refused to refer to him so familiarly. For if she did, all was lost. She was lost.

And so, she remained silent, saying nothing, longing to run her tongue along his finger. To taste him.

"Say it, Pru," he urged, his gaze hot upon her mouth. His finger moved, tracing the fullness of her lower lip, teasing her even further. "Ash. It is so easy to speak, one syllable only. As meaningless as what wood cast into the flame becomes."

She felt as if *she* had been cast into the flame.

For all that she had endured a quarter-hour walk through snow to reach the ruins, with winds buffeting her all the way, there was no lingering trace of coldness in her body now. She was on fire. For him. For the forbidden. For the last man she should ever want.

"I thought you were attempting to help your brother to win my hand," she reminded him. Reminded them both, for that matter.

Not that she intended to marry the Duke of Coventry—indeed, she rather suspected Christabella harbored a *tendre* for the man—but she could not forget what Lord Ashley had told her before. If everything he was doing, every interaction, every word, every seduction, was only being mounted on behalf of his plan to find his brother a duchess, that would be the biggest insult he could pay her. Resisting him would be so easy.

"I have a confession to make," he told her, his stare meshing with hers once more. "Nothing I have said to you—not one bloody word—has had a damn thing to do with winning your hand for my brother. Nor has a single thing I have done. My sole motivation is how badly, how desperately, how uncontrollably I want you, Pru."

Something inside her broke at his confession. Mayhap it

was her defenses. Mayhap it was her ability to reason, to discern right from wrong. But whatever it was, it had been severed as surely as any rope hacked in twain. The last of the ice inside her melted. Her resistance was gone, and in its place was pure, raw hunger.

She tossed her book upon the cushion of the settee, not caring where it went, grasped his waistcoat, rose on her toes, and brought his mouth down to hers.

Chapter Seven

$\mathcal{L}$UST ROARED THROUGH Ash.

Pru was kissing him.

Her mouth was on his. Those soft, sweet, seductive lips he had been denied yesterday in the gardens. The lips he could not stop thinking about. The lips that tormented him in his sleep and his every fantasy. Berry-pink and supple. Plump and tempting.

Those lips were moving against his, with a tentative ardor that undid him.

He had kissed dozens of women in his tenure as a rake-hell. But he had never before experienced a kiss that seduced him. He had always been the seducer. He had been in control. He had been the one to deepen the kiss, to angle his head.

But Pru grabbing him, taking the reins, kissing him first…

It was…

Bloody fucking hell, it was the most delicious, wicked, sensual moment of his entire life. If he walked out the door of this damned feigned ruin and an ill-placed stone promptly fell on his head, he would die a happy man for this one kiss. This one moment with her.

But because there was no ill-placed stone forthcoming, and since he was a greedy bastard when it came to Pru Winter, he never wanted this to end. Her tongue was in his mouth, tentatively seeking, and he could not keep from groaning in satisfaction. Nor could he keep from kissing her back with everything he had.

All the finesse, all the ardor, every rakish trick and technique he had ever learned—he employed them now. Because something had occurred to him this morning as he had ridden away from Gill and Lord Aylesford. And it was that he could not bear to see her married to his brother.

Because she was his.

Prudence Winter was *his*, damn it, and he was going to make her realize the truth, one way or another. And he was going to be the one to marry her. Yes, he bloody well was. If he ever wanted to have more than the income allotted him, and if he ever wanted to have children of his own—a not entirely terrible thought, though he was not certain he wanted the little vagabonds now—he was going to have to wed.

Why not her?

Why not this woman, whose ice turned to sensual, sumptuous fire in his arms?

If it had to be someone, why not the only one who had ever affected him thus? The only one who had ever shaken him to his core? The only one who kissed him as if her very life depended upon it?

He had meant to relay at least half as much to her. To see what she thought of the merit of a proper courtship in deed rather than in lesson. But he had taken one look at her, standing there by the settee, her cheeks rosy from her walk through the cold, wisps of her dark hair curling around her lovely face, and he had forgotten all his good intentions.

Just as he was forgetting them now. Because he was filling his hands with her bottom. One hand on each full, luscious cheek. He cupped them, gave them a gentle squeeze, and drew her even nearer. All the way to his body, until they were pressed together in most indecent, delicious fashion, from hip to chest. Until his cock was buried in the promising curves of her body.

His aching, hard cockstand—the same one he had been sporting in her presence from the second he had first laid eyes on her. He kissed her deeper, moving his tongue against hers, and tasted her. She was so sweet. Her scent was all around him, lush summer blooms, brightness and life and beauty.

Her arms wound around his neck, anchoring him to her. And she was making the sweetest sounds. Little, desperate mewls. He wondered if her nipples were hard. If her cunny was wet.

And then, he banished all thoughts. He decided he did not care. All he did care about was getting more of the woman in his arms. He was ravenous for her. Starved for her, and he could not get enough.

He wanted to give her pleasure.

To make her spend.

Now that he had decided she would be his, a sudden, forceful rush of need washed over him. He was a slave to that desire. To the woman in his arms. He wanted to kiss and lick and touch her everywhere. To learn her body, her needs. To discover what made her wild. He was bursting with the hunger, the curiosity.

Ash tore his lips from hers and ran his open, hungry mouth down the creamy column of her throat. She was even softer here. Even more delicate and feminine. He stopped to worship over the place where her pulse fluttered madly beneath his lips. Here was the purest evidence of her life, that steady thrum, and he was grateful, so grateful for it, for *her*.

He reluctantly released her rump, searching for something else. He required greater access to her, more skin, more everything. Her gown's fastenings were in the back. He found them with ease and began plucking the buttons, one by one.

"Ash," she whispered.

The sigh of his name in her voice was enough to send another arrow of need pulsing through him. Now he had a different problem entirely, the problem of controlling himself and going far enough without going too far and taking her. Because he would not do that.

"Pru," he said, kissing her throat, paying homage to every part of her he could land his mouth upon. All the way to her ear, where he caught the fleshy lobe between his teeth. He licked the whorl, ran his tongue behind it, then back down her neck as she sighed so sweetly.

There was such appreciation in her tone. She was deliciously responsive. In his arms, no seasoned courtesan could hold a candle to her. She was seducing him. Thoroughly. Making him realize that he was hers every bit as much as she was his. Her hands were traveling over him as well, moving over his shoulders, down his arms. And bloody hell, but her tentative caresses made his cock twitch with appreciation.

Still, he forced himself to go slowly. He had waited this long to stake his claim upon Prudence Winter, to work beyond the guilt and the sense of obligation weighing him down. He did not want to rush either of them. By his estimate, they had a good half hour at least before the servant charged with tending the fires returned.

Which meant he was going to prolong this.

He was going to make it good for Pru.

So good she said *yes* when he asked her to marry him.

Here was proof of just how far gone he was: the notion of marriage to Pru did not make him seize with dread. Instead, it made his cock harder. It was as if she had cast a spell upon him. As if she had somehow robbed him of his ability to resist her.

Whatever had changed, there was no undoing it now. The damage had been done. This woman had a power over him no one before her ever had.

He stopped undoing her gown long enough to shrug off his coat, before letting it fall to the floor. His valet would be in an uproar over such a cavalier treatment of the expensive, perfectly tailored garment. He did not have much coin, but what he did have, he spent wisely. It was never said that Lord Ashley Rawdon did not cut a dashing figure.

But either way, Ash did not give a damn. He wanted as few encumbrances as possible between himself and Pru. He was single-minded in his goal. Her bodice gaped. He pulled it down her arms. Stays were in his way, but beneath them, her breasts rose full and lush, hidden from his gaze by her chemise.

Desire roared through him all over again. With her cheeks flushed, her lips swollen from their shared kisses, and delectably disheveled, she was the most erotic sight he had ever beheld. He had to close his eyes for a beat against a frantic surge of need.

"Ash," she said again, her voice hesitant.

An uncertain whisper.

He opened his eyes, drinking her in. "What is it, sweet?"

"This is madness."

"It is," he agreed easily, taking one of her hands in his and holding it over his heart. "Feel this?"

His heart was racing. Galloping as if he had just engaged in some form of sport. All from kissing her. Her hand splayed over his chest, beneath his hand, and even that touch was enough to make him wild. It took every bit of his restraint to keep himself from doing what he longed to do the most—guide her hand lower. Along his abdomen, straight to his cockstand.

But this was not about him. It was about her. About convincing her. Showing her the pleasure he could give her. Demonstrating all the reasons why she had to marry him with the only means of persuasion he possessed. He had always excelled at seduction.

"Your heart is beating fast," she said, her passion-glazed gaze upon his. "Why?"

"It is the effect you have upon me," he admitted.

She swallowed, her lips parting, as if the revelation left her shocked. "Oh."

Surely she had worked suitors before him into such a frenzied state. Pru was a veritable goddess with her delicate beauty, her tall, lush form, those eyes like hot chocolate, that hair he could not help but to imagine free of all its pins, spread over his pillow. Wrapped around his fist.

"Pru," he said then, forcing himself to recall the situation at hand, "do you trust me?"

Because the situation was far bigger than either of them individually. Bigger, even, than the two of them together. It was monumental. Marriage was a lifelong institution.

She took her time answering him, her gaze searching leisurely over his features as if she were not certain of the response she would give him.

"Pru," he pressed, dipping his head toward hers, bringing their foreheads together. "Do you trust me?"

"I do not know," she whispered at last. "I ought not. You are a rake."

To the devil with being a rake.

To the devil with his reputation.

There was more to him, far more to him, than the man he had once been, than the mistakes he had made.

"Perhaps I am a reformed rake now," he offered, rubbing his nose gently over hers. Once, twice. Again.

Damnation, even her nose was silken and delectable. He thought he could happily kiss the tip of it every day. She inhaled sharply at the simple contact, her eyes fluttering closed for a moment. Still, she clutched his shoulders. She did not push him away or bring him nearer.

They were suspended together, by the crackling fire, far away from the many other guests and all the impediments which sought to keep them apart. The rhythmic tinkling against the paned windows suggested the gray skies of earlier had opened up to release tiny shards of ice. But by the fire, in each other's arms, they were warm.

And if it was sleeting, that greatly increased the chance that the servant may be delayed in his return to stoke the fires. It seemed utterly providential.

But Pru had stiffened, and a frown marred her brow. "Reformed rakes do not exist."

"You do not believe a man capable of change?" he asked.

Her tongue ran over her lower lip. He wanted to chase it. To kiss her again. But he knew he could not press her. He had to wait. Feign patience.

"Yes," she allowed.

"Then it stands to reason that rakes can reform themselves." He could not resist caressing her cheek, rubbing his thumb over the proud architecture of her delicate bones. "That you have reformed me."

"What of your brother?" she asked.

Gill.

Fuck.

Not thinking about his brother was easiest. Guilt was ever the killer of ardor, and he still had some, it was true.

But he would not allow her to shake him. "He cannot have you," he growled.

"And neither can you," she said. "You are confusing me

with kisses, wooing me into wickedness. This is what every rake does."

"How many rakes do you know?" he demanded, his tone sharper than he had intended.

A possessive flare surged inside him.

"Only you," she admitted. "And Viscount Aylesford, of course, but he is my sister's betrothed, so he does not count."

"I am not going to ruin you," he vowed. "I promise, Pru. All I want is to give you pleasure."

The dark pupils of her eyes grew larger. "You only want to give me pleasure," she repeated.

"Yes," he said, and then he kissed her again.

Because sometimes actions spoke far more eloquently than words could. He could coax her thus, he was certain of it. And he knew there was nothing complicated about the way she responded to him.

He was rewarded by her melting against him, her lips opening. She was kissing him back. Sucking on his tongue. He nipped her lip. Kissed her harder. Deeper. But he knew he could not seduce her using action alone.

With great reluctance, he tore his mouth from hers once more.

Breathing harshly, he gazed down at her. "I dare you to tell me you do not want me every bit as much as I want you."

"Of course I want you," she admitted, her voice thick. "But that does not mean I will give in to temptation. There is far too much at stake."

That was utter truth.

For there was everything at stake.

But he would prove to her that taking a chance upon him would be worth it.

"Risk it," he dared her.

And then, before she could say another word, he kissed

her again. This time, he deftly loosened her stays. One swift tug, and her breasts sprang free, full and high, trapped beneath the thin barrier of her chemise. He kissed her ear again as he tugged the chemise down.

Another soft moan tore from her lips at the same moment her chemise lowered enough to reveal her breasts. He tongued the hollow beneath her ear before examining his handiwork. Her breasts were on display, pushed up in an erotic offering by the constriction of her lowered undergarments. Creamy and round, tipped with berry-pink nipples that matched her gorgeous mouth, the sight of them sent a throbbing bolt of lust straight to his cock.

He filled his hands with them. They were heavy and full, silken and warm. The lust turned into a desperate hunger. He was voracious for her. Ash lowered his head and sucked a nipple into his mouth.

"Oh," she said on a sigh, and instead of protesting, she threaded her fingers through his hair and arched her back.

Bloody fucking hell.

He played his tongue over the pebbled little bud, gratified when she moaned. She even smelled like summer here, and her breasts were gloriously sensitive. He raked his teeth over her nipple lightly, before drawing her back into his mouth and sucking hard. He was ravenous for her, and needy too, so needy. He could not get enough of the sounds she made, the sensation of her sweet skin.

How had he ever supposed he could woo her for another?

How could he have imagined she could ever be anything other than his?

She felt like his, in his arms. She tasted like his too.

He had to touch her now. Ash grasped a fistful of her gown, petticoat, and chemise, raising it. He moved to her other breast as his hand found the decadent curve of her bare thigh, the sweet place where her stockings ended and there was nothing but Pru's skin on his.

His ballocks were drawn tight.

And he had not even touched her cunny yet.

All the blood in his body seemed to have rushed to his cock. He had never, in all his days, wanted a woman more than he wanted Pru. His fingers found their way between her thighs, parting her soft, slick folds. She was hot and wet. So wet. She wanted him.

It was his turn to moan his approval. He found her pearl, and she jerked. He flicked his tongue over her nipple as he stimulated her, slowly at first. Nothing more than gentle, slow circles. Her breathy gasp told him she liked his touch. So he went faster. Stroked the swollen bud, working his fingers over it.

He was attuned to her every sigh, her every soft mewl, to the rocking of her hips, the way she shifted to grant him greater access to her, to the tightening of her fingers in his hair. Because he was going mindless with the need to pleasure her, to make her come, to give her the sweet rush of release, to stake his claim, he bit her nipple and increased his pace. More moisture bathed his fingertips.

Her essence.

He could not wait to suck his fingers clean.

To taste her there.

But they had time. The rest of their lives. This was just the beginning.

He kissed his way back to her lips, over her breasts, up the sleek column of her neck. And then his mouth was on hers once more. This kiss was deeper than all that had come before. It was laden with carnal promise. With acknowledgement, too. How badly he longed to sink a finger inside her sheath. To replace it with his cock.

Slowly, he reminded himself, stroking her pearl, his tongue sliding inside her mouth. She clung to him, kissing him, and in the next instant, her body stiffened. She cried out, tremors quaking through her as she spent. He swallowed her cry, relentlessly working her until a second, smaller orgasm shuddered through her. Until she was gasping and limp in his arms.

Then, and only then, did he remove his fingers from her sweet cunny, allowing her skirts to fall. He broke the kiss and could not resist sucking the fingers he had just used to pleasure her into his mouth as she watched. Her lust-drunk eyes widened. The taste of her, summery and sweet, musky and earthy, blossomed on his tongue.

Next time, he would taste her truly, lick her until she screamed.

"God, Pru," he managed. "You are so sweet. Sweeter than I could have imagined."

His words seemed to serve as a return to reality for her, and he instantly wished he could recall them, for her brow furrowed, and she froze.

"This was wrong," she said softly. "You are dallying with me, Lord Ashley."

She could not be further from the truth.

"I promise you I do not dally with you," he vowed, determined to keep her here with him. Determined to keep her in his arms for as long as he possibly could.

Her frown deepened, however. "What are you suggesting? Forgive me, but I fail to see how continually seeking me out, kissing me, undoing my bodice, and…doing what you have just done is anything other than dallying with me."

"I want to marry you," he bit out.

And instantly wished he could recall those words.

Poorly done of him.

He had meant to rehearse. Had intended to seduce her, to make her spend, and then offer her his proposition while the sated glow still infected her mind and she could not manage to form her lips into a *no* when he asked her to be his wife.

"You want to marry me," she repeated, her tone dazed.

This, too, was a mistake, he thought. Not the proposal itself, but the manner in which he had made it.

He grimaced. "Yes, though I was hoping to do better with my proposal than that."

"You no longer want me to marry the duke," she said slowly, "because you wish to marry me yourself."

"Yes." Although when she said it thus, it truly sounded horrid. "Yes, of course. You cannot imagine I would be cad enough to touch you and then see you wed to my brother."

What an arse he was. It had all seemed so simple earlier on his ride. Even on his walk here. He had arrived with purpose, with determination, a bloody battle plan. And then he had taken one look at her and had turned into a ravening beast. He wanted to plant himself a facer.

"Thank you, but no," she said calmly.

And then she extricated herself from his embrace before spinning about and presenting him with her back. She shimmied, righting her stays and chemise, pulling them back into their proper places. He stared at the buttons he had plucked from their moorings, at the tantalizing swath of creamy skin he had unveiled with his efforts. Her shoulders were elegant and beautiful, and from this angle, her neck was perfection. Made for his lips.

He stood there, dumbfounded.

Utterly astounded.

Realization crept over him, slowly at first, and then like a pail of water fetched from the icy waters of the serpentine lake here at Abingdon Hall. She had refused him twice over. First, his advances. And then, his proposal of marriage.

Impossible. No woman had ever turned him down. Not when it came to lovemaking, that was. He had certainly never asked another to marry him.

"No?" he repeated. It seemed to be all he could say, a foolish echo of her denial.

Her refusal. Her outright rejection.

"No," she said agreeably, casting a look at him over her shoulder. "Would you mind repairing the damage you have done, my lord? I fear I cannot reach all the buttons on my own."

She was so nonchalant. So composed. And he was…

Not. Decidedly not.

But he did as she asked, slipping the buttons into their homes one by one.

"Why?" he asked when he was halfway through with his task. It seemed the obvious answer. "Why not? What is so damned bad about the notion of being my wife?"

"I have already told you, I have no wish to marry," she said. "If you had been honest with me from the first, I could have spared you this merry chase. But instead, you chose to mislead me and pretend you were attempting to win me over for your brother, when all along you were merely trying to seduce me into marrying you."

She had that all wrong.

He slid the last button home. "Pru, that is not what happened. Everything I told you was true."

She whirled around to face him, anger flashing in her eyes. "Do you dare to expect me to believe that? What a tidy way of solving your financial woes. Do not think for a moment I am not aware Coventry needs to marry a wealthy woman. Why would you, the second son, be any different? But the two of you colluded to land yourselves brides, did you not? You settled upon me, and he upon Christabella. I should have seen it before now. Indeed I credited myself with possessing more intelligence than this."

"That is not the way of it," he said, attempting to explain himself—if he could.

What a muck he had made of things. This cozy interlude in the ruins was meant to have led to pleasure and her acquiescence. Not her outrage.

"Do not," she snapped, "say another word more, Lord Ashley. I have heard more than enough lies from you. Enough to last me a lifetime."

She spun away from him, hurrying away to where her pelisse, hat and muff had been carefully hung by the door. He watched helplessly as she donned her outerwear, her face an icy mask, and then stormed from the room.

"Damnation," he muttered to himself, wondering how he had gone so dreadfully wrong.

It had all been going so well…

Something caught his attention then. Something quite curious indeed.

It seemed Pru had left behind her book.

PRU FLED.

It was becoming something of an unfortunate habit since Lord Ashley Rawdon had entered her life. The blustery wind assailed her, sending sleet into her face. She held her muffler in one hand and her skirts and pelisse in the other as she frantically trudged along the path, back toward Abingdon House. She had not bothered to see if he chased after her. If he chose, she had no doubt he could catch up to her in no time, with his long-legged strides unencumbered by a gown and petticoats.

But she was too angry too care.

Angry with him.

Angry with herself.

Hot tears of humiliation stung her eyes, blurring her vision along with the sleet pelting her. How easily she had been led into being a rakehell's prey. All it required was a handsome face, a charming grin, nimble fingers, and knowing kisses, and she had nearly been his.

How had she ever allowed herself to believe a word that man had uttered? He had convinced her he was aiding his socially awkward, perpetually quiet brother in finding a wife. What a paragon he had seemed, so caring, so concerned for his brother's future. And then, when his true motives had begun to show after that first kiss, she had allowed herself to become swept up in his skilled seductions.

She had kissed him back.

Had been tempted by him.

Had spent the last week longing for him, at war with herself over the way he made her feel. Because wanting him was dangerous and selfish and foolish…

Stupid, as it turned out. So horribly, unutterably stupid.

"Pru!"

His voice rang out. The slamming of the door to the false ruins echoed through the little copse of pine trees surrounding it. She turned back to find him trudging through the snow after her. His head was bare, and he was not even wearing his greatcoat. Nothing but shirtsleeves and waistcoat to defend his skin from the punishing sleet and cold winter's air.

For a moment, she actually felt sorry for him.

And then she remembered what a manipulative scoundrel he was. Why, he had nearly removed her gown all whilst kissing her. He was more skilled than any lady's maid she had ever known, the wretched rogue.

"Leave me alone, you cad!" she hollered at him before continuing to make her miserable journey back to the main house.

But to make matters worse, she attempted to run too quickly, and her boots slid on the fresh coating of ice pellets over snow. She lost her balance, waving her arms like a Bedlamite, and went down like a sack of flour. Her bottom slammed hard into the packed gravel of the path, with nothing to pad her fall save a small layer of icy snow.

Pain shot through her, and she clenched her teeth against it.

"Pru, my God, have you hurt yourself?" demanded the rake she had been running from.

Part of her wanted to believe the concern in his voice was real, but then she pushed that notion away, reminding herself that nothing about him was true. It was all one big, deliberate act. Seduce the eldest Winter daughter, the long Meg, the one no one else wants.

Another wave of misery crashed upon her.

Pru was aware of what everyone said about her. About how awkward it was to be the tallest female in the chamber, and a wicked Winter as well. How could she have allowed him to make her feel wanted? To fool her into believing a beautiful man like him would actually desire her?

"Go away!" she yelled at him, doing her best not to cry.

She allowed herself a stunned moment of remaining where she was, because the agony of her pain—both physical and emotional—was too great to bear. But then her pride roared to the fore, telling her she was Pru Winter, damn it. And she did not wallow in her misery for any man.

Not even the second son of a duke.

Especially not Lord Ashley Rawdon.

Her palms burned as she flattened them on the ice and snow to leverage herself back into a standing position. Her muffler was gone, her hat knocked desperately askew in her pitiful plunge. The sleet only seemed to come down harder, adding to her dejection.

And then, he was there. Of course, he was, the rotten knave.

His big, warm hands took hold of hers, and she hated how comforting they felt. How much she relished that touch. Would she never learn her lesson? Gently, he helped her to her feet. He was frowning down at her, his gaze searching.

"Pru, what did you hurt?" he asked.

She rather thought it was her heart. It was most definitely her pride. A twinge of pain sliced through her once more, reminding her of yet another reason why being too tall was a hindrance rather than a boon: the higher the height, the greater the fall.

"I am perfectly well," she muttered, blinking away her tears. "Do go away, Lord Ashley. I have already endured more of you than I can bear."

"You are in pain," he observed grimly, giving her hands a gentle squeeze. "That was quite a fall you took."

"It was nothing," she argued for the sake of her pride, which was just as foolish as the rest of her, it would seem.

He had to be cold, with the sleet and the wind driving into him, and yet he seemed only to be worried over her welfare. Doubt crept into her heart, making her wonder if he was indeed that fine an actor, or if all was not exactly as she had deemed it.

Before she could further argue the matter, he bent and swept her into his arms. She gasped, her arms going around his neck for purchase. She had to be heavy, given her height. And yet, he made her feel dainty. His grim countenance showed nary a hint of strain.

"Put me down," she protested, because she knew the last thing she should be doing was remaining in his presence, giving him a chance to worm his way back into her good graces and convince her she had been wrong.

But her backside was still smarting, and being in his arms felt good. Her traitorous body had yet to realize what a blackguard he was. For that matter, so had much of the rest of her.

"I am carrying you back inside, where I can have a look at your injuries for myself," he informed her, pivoting in the snow with a graceful ease she only wished she had exhibited earlier.

But of course, she had gone sprawling to her doom. And of course he had scooped her up like some sort of gallant swain. And of course her stupid heart was pounding faster, and not even the merciless ice and cold could diminish the unwanted heat roiling through her in answer to the glory of being in Lord Ashley Rawdon's arms.

Even if he was a rakehell with a heart of stone.

Belatedly, it occurred to her that her injury was on her derriere. He could hardly look at that. How mortifying.

"I can walk on my own, Lord Ashley," she argued once more. "Let me go."

"No," he insisted stubbornly. "I shall not run the risk of you falling again and hurting yourself worse. This snow is dreadfully slippery with the sleet now lying upon it."

"What if you fall?" she could not resist asking. "I should think it would be far safer if you were to allow me to go on my own. If you take the both of us down—"

"Pru," he interrupted. "Stop talking. Nothing you say will change a bloody thing. I am carrying you. Stop being so stubborn."

Pru was not even the most stubborn of the Winters. That title belonged to her sister, Grace. But further quarreling with him was a moot point, because they had reached the front door to the ruins once more. Lord Ashley exhibited a remarkable amount of dexterity, opening it with one hand, all while never letting her go or so much as shifting her in his arms.

And then, they were back inside the great hall of the ruins, out of the freezing sleet that had been pelting them. The door slammed shut. It was eerily quiet, save for the fire at the far end of the hall, decorated with holly garlands. It crackled on.

Pru and Lord Ashley stared at each other. Their faces were inexorably close. One tip of her chin, one slight movement, and they would be kissing again. She shivered, but the reaction was only partially due to the cold.

He took note. "You must feel like ice after that spill."

"I am perfectly warm," she lied.

In truth, wetness from the snow and sleet was seeping through her skirts and petticoats. She was beginning to realize they were quite sodden. She shuddered again, unable to stay the instinctive reaction.

"Obstinate fool," he muttered.

And then he was stalking once more, still holding her in his arms. They were back in the room from which she had run not long before. He settled her upon the oversized cushion of the settee. Thank heavens the piece of furniture was remarkably well-upholstered, for her bottom was still sore.

Before she could protest, he sank to his knees before her, parting her pelisse and clasping handfuls of her snow-laden hem in his hands. "Good God, Pru. Your gown is covered in snow. You will be drenched when it melts. Do tell me what hurts, if you please. Is it your ankle? Something else?"

"It is nothing," she forced herself to say. "I have already told you more than once, I am well. All I wish is to be left alone. To be free of your intolerable presence at last."

"Are you certain you find me intolerable?" the scoundrel dared to ask, as he lifted her skirts higher, revealing her stocking-clad calves above her smart boots. "It did not seem so earlier, when you were kissing me."

"That was before I realized what you wanted from me," she said coldly, reaching down to swat at his hands. "Get your hands off my hem, my lord. And do cease lifting my skirts at once."

"Wanting you as my wife is such a great crime?" he asked, ignoring her and lifting her skirts even higher, all the way to her knees.

He settled the snow-crusted hem back down upon the floor. There was a draft in the chamber, and it licked at her already-chilled skin, making her shudder again.

"You are cold, regardless of all your insistence that you are not," he observed drily. "Do you suppose there are any blankets in this wretched place?"

Truly, she did not know. But it occurred to her that if he went off in search of them, she would at least be afforded a few minutes of solace. Time enough to gather her wits. Time enough to attempt a second escape.

"In one of the other chambers," she lied. "Yes, I do believe so."

He pinned a narrowed gaze upon her. "I will be back in a trice. Do not move, Pru. I will only catch you again, and bring you back here until you are safe and warm."

But there was the crux of the problem. She was not safe with him. Not at all. Indeed, she was in the greatest danger of her life. Because he was a heartless rake with a charming air, wicked lips, and a kiss that could not help but to seduce.

Whilst she was the feather-brained fool he wanted to marry for her dowry.

"I will remain precisely where I am." She felt not a hint of shame when she fibbed once more.

Her mind was already plotting her next battle plan...

He rose to his formidable height and stalked across the chamber.

The moment he crossed the threshold, she would rise and make another attempt at fleeing the false ruins. If he was preoccupied enough, he would not even hear her make a sound...

"Ah, how fortuitous," he said then, breaking through her concentration with his deep, delicious voice.

Her gaze jerked to him. He held a fur blanket aloft, which he had apparently plucked from behind a nearby chair. She ought to have known she could not be fortunate enough to escape him.

"Fortuitous indeed," she agreed through clenched teeth.

But it was his next words, as he returned to her side, that truly alarmed her.

He tossed the fur blanket to the settee alongside her. "I am afraid we are going to have to get you out of that wet pelisse and gown, Pru. There is no other way to keep you from taking a chill."

Chapter Eight

$\mathscr{A}$SH TOOK PRU'S hands in his, trying to ignore the surge of pure, unadulterated need rushing through him at the mere touch of her bare skin to his. For this was not about seduction at all. Rather, this was about tending to her. Taking care of her.

Apologizing for his blockheaded proposal with deed rather than words. Perhaps she would find those more useful. Christ knew he always had.

He drew her to a standing position once more, and then he made short work of her pelisse. His fingers navigated the familiar path of the buttons lining the back of her modest bodice.

"Lord Ashley, this is beyond improper," she remonstrated, but her tone lacked conviction.

It was deuced difficult to sound angry when one was shivering. And she was certainly doing that. He had been the one stripped to his shirtsleeves out in the biting wind and sleet, but her tumble into the snow had wreaked its havoc upon her.

Her minimal resistance was proof of that.

"The time for fretting over what is proper and what is not is long gone between us, Pru," he told her, intent upon his course.

There was no desire to woo in him now. This was not the

manner in which he had believed—in all his naïve suppositions on his morning ride—he would seduce Pru Winter into becoming his wife. Not once had he imagined his bungled proposal, her refusal, her flight and subsequent fall, and then his rescue of her.

He was not accustomed to playing Sir Galahad.

But for her, he was beginning to discover, he would gladly undertake any number of firsts. For her—to win her—he would go to greater lengths than he had ever gone for another.

"You will not cozen me into marrying you no matter what you do," she warned, teeth clacking together.

"I have no wish to cozen you," he said truthfully, wondering just how many damned buttons she had on this cursed gown. It had not seemed so many earlier, when his lips had been all over her beautiful skin.

"No more lies, my lord," she said, half plea, half command.

He stilled in his task, meeting her gaze once more. "No lies," he agreed.

And he meant those words, oh, how he meant them.

Because the strangest realization had hit him, rather with the force of a lightning strike, in the moment after she had run from him. He had discovered her book—*The Tale of Love*—of course, just as he had expected all along. Finite proof: Pru Winter had a wicked side. She was curious. Curious enough to have such a forbidden, bawdy book in her possession. Curious enough to be reading it.

And a new fire had ignited within him.

But the fire had not just been passion.

Rather, it had been—and here, he would have once shuddered with disgust—*love*. Only now, there was no shuddering. There was only acceptance. Shocked acceptance, but acceptance nonetheless.

How strange, how foreign that unwanted emotion seemed now as he faced a rather bedraggled-looking Pru in the wake of her fall. She was coated in a dusting of snow and ice. Her brunette locks had drips of water clinging to them like tiny stars. She was pale, her lips pale too, shivering.

Gorgeous.

Unlike any woman whose acquaintance he had ever made. She was tall and lovely, fierce and feisty, proper yet wicked. She matched him, wit for wit, kiss for kiss. And there was no other word to describe the strange feeling, deep in the darkest pit of his stomach, whenever he was in her presence. Whenever he thought about her.

He was in love.

But he could hardly tell her that now, because he had already done such a poor job of proposing that he had sent her running as if she fled a burning building with her hair on fire. He was responsible for the nasty fall she had taken. And if he did not take action, she was going to take ill with a lung infection before he could even bother to make his grand declaration.

"I am not removing my gown," she announced around another shiver.

"You are correct, sweet," he said, as he began to pull her arms from her sleeves. "I am removing it for you."

"You are not removing it either," she argued, ever prideful.

This time, he could hear her teeth chattering together.

Blast.

He ignored her and drew it over her head. "There, now. I just have. No more arguing, if you please."

"Vexing man," she muttered.

All the fight seemed to drain from her then, and she allowed him to make quick work of her petticoat and stays.

She stood before him, clad in nothing more than her chemise. And it was transparent. *Lord, God.* He forgot how to swallow for a moment as he took in the hint of her dusky nipples, puckered and stiff, poking the fabric, and the shadow at the apex of her thighs.

But then, her teeth started to chatter once more, and he was reminded of the reason he had just disrobed her. Which was not to ogle her, regardless of how mouthwatering the sight of Pru in chemise only truly was.

He urged her to sit, and then tucked the fur all around her before dropping to his knees once more. Her boots were covered in snow, and he would wager her toes were freezing within, since she wore nothing more than her stockings beneath, even if they were thick winter stockings.

"What are you doing now?" she protested weakly, but she made no effort to move her feet.

Instead, she snuggled deeper into the settee, wrapping the fur more firmly about herself. He quickly undid her boots and pulled them off. Her stockinged feet were cold and wet as he held them in his hands to warm them.

"Your toes are like ice," he said. "It is a damned good thing I carried you back here, Pru. It is far too cold out for you to be worried over your pride."

"Oh," she said on a soft little sigh that sent a bolt of lust straight through him. "That does feel so much better, Lord Ashley."

He squeezed her toes, then rubbed each foot tenderly between his hands, trying to warm her as best as he could. Ash did not think he had ever before taken note of a lady's feet. Certainly, he had never taken the time to stop and admire them with past lovers. And yet, he could not help but to find even Pru's feet entrancing. They were dainty and small in his hands, her ankles perfectly curved, and leading to calves that were mostly hidden beneath the fur.

But he knew from his initial attempt to discern where she had injured herself in her fall that her calves were sleek and gorgeous. Just like the rest of her. Every part of this woman intrigued him. There was not one bit of her he did not find utterly mesmerizing.

"Do your toes feel warmer, sweet?" he forced himself to ask through a voice gone thick with desire.

"Yes," she murmured. "Much warmer now, thank you."

"Excellent." He tucked the fur around them, and then he stood.

That was when he made his second realization of the day, and quite belatedly. He, too, was soaked. Because he had pursued her in nothing but his shirtsleeves, the lawn of his shirt was now chilled and sticking to his skin. His breeches were wet, as were his boots.

There was no hope for it. He was going to have to strip himself of his sodden garments and join her beneath the fur. Naturally, the prospect held its own appeal.

He opened the buttons of his waistcoat, his eyes on her. "My clothing is soaked as well. We will have to huddle together beneath the fur while our garments dry by the fire.

Her eyes went wide. "You…are taking off your shirt?"

"Yes," he said agreeably, hoping the prospect made her at least feel even a modicum of the longing coursing through him for her. "And my breeches as well."

"Your breeches?" The last emerged from her as a squeak.

He could not stifle his grin. "That is what I just said, sweet."

"But you cannot," she said, once more back to her proper self now that she was warming.

"On the contrary. I can, and I will. You may, of course, avert your gaze as it pleases you." He shucked his waistcoat and carried it to the fire along with her garments, laying them neatly on the hearth in an effort to dry them. "But you need not fear my modesty, Pru. I do not mind if you look."

"I will do nothing of the sort," she denied.

He cast her a knowing glance. "As you wish." And then he hauled his shirt over his head.

When he had removed it, she was still staring at him, her eyes devouring his torso. Ash knew what the hunger in her gaze meant. He had seen it before. She found his chest appealing. Here, at last, was a sign that she was not as unaffected and disapproving as she would like to pretend.

Thank God, because he was still determined to make her his bride. He would simply go on wooing her and persuading her until he earned a *yes* from those delectable lips instead of a polite *no thank you*.

He stoked the fire, then, all too aware of how symbolic the act was. If only success with Pru was as easy to achieve. But though he had not convinced her yet, he possessed two traits that would serve him well now: patience and persistence.

And he had no qualms about putting both—not to mention his body—to use in aiding his quest to make Pru Winter his, once and for all.

PRU TOLD HERSELF to look away.

And then she licked her suddenly dry lips, allowing her gaze to roam over the bare expanse of Lord Ashley's back as he tended the fire. The flames burned higher and hotter. So, too her cheeks and the answering burst of need she could never quite quell.

Her ire was fast fading. Perhaps it was the effect of the cold leaching from her body. She was cozy and comfortable tucked into the fur. And try as she might to hold on to her vexation with him, she could not help but to recall the way he had rushed to her rescue. The way he had carried her in his arms, back into the ruins. The feeling of his large hands on her feet, the manner in which he had completely ignored his own chill in favor of warming her first.

None of these were the acts of a scoundrel.

Rather, they were the acts of a gentleman. Which was truly confusing, because she had already decided upon precisely who and what Lord Ashley Rawdon was before she had run from his proposal and his passionate kisses both.

He frightened her, it was true. Not because he was half a head taller than she, with a broad, strong body that towered over hers. Not because he was strong, as evidenced by his carrying her through the snow and the muscles rippling in his back even now. Not because he was a rake.

But because of her reaction to him, because of the way he made her feel on the inside. It was the first time she had ever been beset by such marrow-deep longing, such desperate, aching need. And she did not know what to do with those feelings or how to ignore them, unless she was as far from him as she could possibly get.

Here and now, in the fire-bathed warmth of the false ruins, he was alarmingly near. And he was about to get nearer still.

Her cheeks were flaming as he glanced over his shoulder at her and sent her a smile. A true smile, slow and steady, revealing one dimple in his cheek. He looked so different for that heart-stopping moment, so painfully beautiful. She could not control the stab of pure desire that smile sent to her core. Nor could she keep herself from smiling back at him.

With the fire glowing and crackling behind him, he seemed almost golden. Like some mythical god descended from the heavens to tempt mortals to sin. To tempt her.

It was working.

"I thought you said you would not look," he teased softly.

Her flush heightened, and she swore it reached the tips of her ears. "I was looking at the fire, my lord," she lied.

"And do you approve?" he asked her, setting aside the poker before he stood and turned to face her. "Of the fire, that is?"

The fire.

The only fire she was aware of in that instant was the one raging through her blood.

She swallowed with great difficulty, trying not to notice the chiseled ridges of his abdomen or the well-defined muscles of his chest. His torso was long and lean, just like the rest of him. Without his coat and waistcoat, his legs were on loving display, clad in nothing more than his breeches and boots.

"The fire seems adequate," she told him.

"Just adequate?"

There was an edge to his voice. She was goading him, and she knew it. But she could not seem to stop. She was not speaking about the fire. She could not even bring herself to tear her gaze from Lord Ashley's masculine form long enough to give the flames he had just stoked any notice.

"Satisfactory," she amended, although she knew she ought not. But teasing him was enjoyable, even if he still had her at sixes and sevens over his actions.

"I am not sure I like satisfactory any more than I liked adequate," he said, and then bent to remove his own boots.

How intimate it was, how strange to watch him undress.

How wicked.

How wonderful.

Still burrowed beneath the fur, she could not seem to wrest her gaze from him. Until his long, elegant fingers reached the fall of his breeches, and he began plucking the buttons from their moorings.

"What are you doing, my lord?" she demanded. "You cannot remove your breeches!"

"They are wet," he told her firmly, as calmly as if they were engaging in a casual drawing room conversation. "They need to dry along with the rest of our garments."

He had neatly laid out their boots and clothing before the fire, though she had somehow failed to take note before now, ogling him as she had been. What a dreadful weakness she had for this man.

But she still had the presence of mind to recall the ramifications of being in dishabille together. Even if nothing untoward should occur, there was nothing more damning than an unwed lady and an unwed gentleman stripped down to their undergarments.

"If we are caught together thus, I will be compromised," she managed to say past her foolishly thudding heart.

Here was the crux of her quarrel with him, she reminded herself. He wanted to marry her. Likely to get his hands on her share of the Winter fortune. She did not want to marry anyone. Most especially not a disarming rake.

"If I do not get these sodden breeches off and get beneath that fur with you, I will be fighting off a lung infection of my own," he countered, reaching the last button on his falls. "Unless you want to be responsible for my demise, sweet, I suggest you forget your notion of propriety."

She bit her lip and averted her gaze at the last possible second, just before he began tugging the breeches down his hips. Everything was even hotter, just knowing he was disrobing. The sound of the fabric sliding down his legs alone was enough to have her squirming uncomfortably beneath the heavy warmth of the fur.

"I do not want to be responsible for your demise, my lord," she told him, at last finding her voice. "I am sure there is an endless list of ladies who would mourn you."

She had not meant the last to emerge with bitterness, but somehow, it did.

"There is only one lady I would wish to mourn me," he said, and then he was sliding beneath the fur alongside her, his large body crowding her in a way she liked too much. "You."

His words shocked her almost as much as his presence did.

She turned to him, startled at the proximity of his face to hers. They were touching, hip to hip. And his mouth was far too close a temptation. She tried to regain herself, to be stern. Had she not told herself, at the onset of this madness, that she could control her mind even if she could not control her reaction to him?

When had her mind become as unruly as the rest of her?

The answer came to her swiftly as she fell headlong into his startlingly clear blue gaze. She took note, once more, of the rich hues buried within the depths of his eyes: gray, green, and violet circling the obsidian discs of his pupils. The blue was truly a blend of at least a dozen other colors. At once so simple and yet deeply complicated.

Much like the way she felt for him.

"Have I shocked you?" he asked, his voice, like his expression, almost tender.

"You are charming me again," she said.

He studied her intently. "Have I *ever* charmed you, Pru Winter?"

Only every second she spent in and out of his presence.

"You have certainly tried, I believe," she said instead of admitting the troubling truth.

He leaned toward her, so near his nose nearly brushed

hers and their foreheads almost touched. His breath fell hot upon her lips, an almost-kiss. "Now for the true question, the only one which matters. Have I succeeded?"

Of course he had. He was now, drat him. She had just done her best to escape him and his maddening presence and the confusion he had created inside her. But he had dragged her back into his web of silken seduction.

"Why are you doing this?" she asked, searching his gaze for the answer she sought.

A slight smile curved his lips. "Why am I doing what, sweet?"

Her heart gave a pang at his endearment. She firmly banished it, summoning up her resolve. "Any of this. It all began with you following me. Why?"

"I told you the truth that day, Pru," he told her solemnly, before a shudder went through him. "My brother wanted to make you his duchess, but he is dreadful at talking to the fairer sex. I thought ease the waters. We had a wager, you see, that I could help him secure the bride of his choosing."

"You were following me because of a wager," she repeated.

He had the grace to look shamefaced. "Yes. But, it did not take me long to realize there was no chance of me allowing you to wed my brother, regardless of how much I love him."

"How noble," she commented acidly. "You truly expect me to believe this, my lord?"

He shrugged, shivering once more. "It is the truth, Pru."

He was cold. Because he had chased after her. And he had tended to her first.

She sighed, knowing what she was about to do went against her better judgment. "You may scoot nearer to me if you wish. I am significantly warmer than you are, I would wager."

"That would not be proper," he pointed out instead of

instantly sidling nearer as she had supposed he would.

But then his teeth gave a little chatter.

Part of her was not certain if this was another of his rakish ruses. Either way, she felt responsible for his chill. She moved closer herself, hesitating for a moment before placing her arms around him.

She ground her molars against the sensation of his bare skin beneath her fingertips. He was smooth and yet contained such barely leashed power. It was a delightful juxtaposition— the sleekness of his flesh coupled with masculine, corded muscles.

"I do believe we are beyond proper," she observed grimly. "And you are cold because of me. It is only fair if I do my part to warm you after you made certain I did not turn into an icicle."

"I can think of other ways to warm me," he said.

Her head snapped back so she could see his face. He was grinning at her, the rogue, revealing that lone dimple. Looking like that glorious golden god once more, the one she could not resist. He was teasing her, she realized.

"You are a scoundrel," she returned, but her insult lacked heat.

"A terrible one," he agreed easily.

Still, she was not sure that he actually was. At least not to the degree she had supposed when she had gone running into the snow and ice. Her reaction to his proposal earlier had been partially down to her wounded pride. Now, she was no longer as certain as she had been earlier that everything had been a lie. He certainly seemed truthful when he offered his explanation.

"You are telling me the truth about your brother, Lord Ashley?" she pressed.

Why did he have to smell so good? Feel so good? Look so

good? Why did he have to be caring and considerate and tender? Not wanting him would be so much easier if he were a wretch. If his body did not feel so delicious beneath her traveling hands. And traveling they were, much to her dismay, over his back and shoulders, down his arms. Caresses, in truth. She told herself it was the best means of warming his cool skin.

"Of course I am telling you the truth," he said, his voice a deep vibration she absorbed with her fingertips. "I have told you nothing but the truth from the moment... Fair enough. I did tell you several lies."

She stilled. "What were they?"

"I lied about following you that day in the library," he said, his voice unrepentant. "The truth is, I had been following you."

Pru frowned at him. "I already knew that."

"I also lied about Coventry's interest in foundling hospitals," he admitted. "I never heard him speak of them. But I would like to do penance for that lie now. I want to hear about the foundling hospital that is so dear to you, and about the one you imagine yourself running one day."

Yet again, she searched his gaze, looking for a sign of deceit. He seemed genuine, however. Earnest.

"What do you want to know about it?" she asked.

His arm slid around her waist, drawing her more firmly to his side. She settled there, allowing the closeness, the intimacy. This time, it felt right. Natural.

Better than natural.

It felt good.

"Everything there is to know about it," he said softly. "Tell me about the children there. What are they like?"

She smiled to think of them. "Oh, how I miss them. They are lonely, so many of them. They are desperate for someone to embrace them, to show them affection. I play games with them. Some, I have been teaching to read. Others, the infants, are the sweetest. I hold them when their wet nurses have finished their feeding if I am able."

There was nothing sweeter than an innocent baby nestling in one's arms. Pru loved children, and when her brother had begun the foundling hospital, she had realized just how meaningful she found her interactions with them. Knowing the children there had no families of their own broke her heart. How she wished she could take them all under her wing and claim each as her own.

"You care about them," Lord Ashley said then, interrupting her thoughts.

"Very much so," she agreed, her smile turning sad. "I miss them, whilst I am here in the country."

"I admire that, Pru." His voice was even quieter than it had been before. "More than you know."

For some odd reason, she found herself believing him.

Chapter Nine

*T*HIS WAS NOT the first occasion upon which Ash had opened his eyes to find an irate gentleman hovering over him, wearing a murderous scowl. It was, however, the first time the homicidal gentleman in question was the *brother* of the lady in dishabille at his side instead of the husband.

He blinked, hoping he was having a nightmare.

Then blinked again.

Damnation, Mr. Devereaux Winter was still hovering over him, looking as if he wanted to sink a blade between his ribs. Or plant him a facer. Perhaps both. Simultaneously.

"Is something in your eye, Rawdon?" growled his host.

Ash ceased blinking. The lady in his arms stirred, making sweet little murmurings of wakefulness, which otherwise would have had his cock standing at attention. Given the circumstances, he would be bloody fortunate if his cock had not shriveled up and retracted inside his body, terrified it was about to be hacked off by the brute staring him down.

"Nothing is in my eye, Mr. Winter," he forced himself to say, amazed at how smoothly the words emerged, quite as if he had not a care.

Quite as if he were not wearing nothing more than his smalls whilst Devereaux's innocent, unwed sister was curled up in his embrace, clad in only a transparent chemise. He could still recall every aching detail of just how translucent the curst garment was with perfect clarity.

"If you do not take your paws off my sister in the next ten seconds, there *will* be something in your eye," promised his host, his voice undeniably menacing. "My bloody fist."

Fucking hell.

He eyed Devereaux's enormous hands, which were already clenched into fists.

Pru was still half asleep, settled deliciously into his body. But she stirred more at the barely suppressed violence in her brother's tone. He hated to wake her completely and put an end to the unexpected intimacy they had shared here in the false ruins—so very unlike any intimacy he had ever experienced before with a woman in that it had involved nothing more than an embrace and conversation. But he was going to have to, or her brother was going to murder him.

And Ash did not blame the irate fellow one whit. For if Pru were his sister, and he discovered her unclothed and asleep in the arms of a rakehell such as himself, he would assume the worst.

"This is not what it seems, Devereaux," he said. And then he gave Pru a gentle nudge. "Pru, sweet, wake."

"*Pru?*" Repeated his host, outraged. "*Sweet?*"

The last term of endearment emerged as a bellow, which served to wake Pru better than Ash's halfhearted attempts had. She jolted upright with a squeal, her head knocking into Ash's chin as she did so, with enough force that his eyes watered with the pain.

He supposed it served him right.

"Serves you right," grunted Devereaux. "I hope you bit your damned tongue right off."

Ash rubbed his chin ruefully. There would be no sympathy from his host. Nor any quarter, it would seem.

"Fortunately, it is still intact," he managed to inform Pru's outraged brother. "Again, Mr. Winter, I regret the tableau you have happened upon—"

"I did not happen upon it," seethed Winter, interrupting him. "One of my servants did."

Pru gasped then, finally awake enough to grasp what was unfolding around them. "Nothing untoward occurred, Dev. Lord Ashley was a perfect gentleman."

Winter's brows shot upward. "Ah, I see. Then my eyes are deceiving me, and those are not your garments strewn about the hearth, along with Lord Ashley's? And you are not sitting indecently near to him and sharing a fur blanket?"

Pru winced. Ashley grimaced.

"That is all true, Mr. Winter," he said needlessly, attempting to mollify the bear, if he could. "However, there is a reason for the state in which you have found us. Miss Winter fell and injured herself in the snow. I brought her back here so she could warm herself lest she catch a lung infection. However, by the time we reached the ruins, both our garments were soaked. I laid them by the fire to dry."

Naturally, he neglected to mention the portion of the story involving Pru fleeing from his proposal. No need to completely humiliate himself, after all.

"He is telling you the truth, Dev," Pru added. "Lord Ashley was kind enough to come to my rescue."

"He also ruined you," Mr. Winter announced, more somber than an executioner.

Blast.

As much as Ash wanted to marry Pru and make her his forever, these were not the words he wanted to hear. He wanted to earn Pru's love and trust. To win her hand. To wed her because it was what she wanted, not because it was what they were forced into doing.

"He did nothing at all to me, Dev," Pru stubbornly insisted. "We huddled together for warmth, and we shared conversation. That was all."

But then Winter reached inside his coat and extracted the most damning evidence of all, holding it aloft. The gilt title emblazoned on the leather cover was undeniable. *The Tale of Love.*

"Perhaps you would care to explain the presence of this outrage," Winter said, his tone deceptively calm.

Bloody hell, Ash had forgotten all about Pru's bawdy book. He had been so caught up in their conversation that he had not even bothered to hide it. Like an utter fool, he had simply allowed it to lay in plain sight where anyone could find it. Much as he had fallen asleep with Pru half-naked in his arms where anyone could find the both of them.

And where they had.

"The book is mine," he said.

"It is my book," Pru announced in unison.

Still rubbing his smarting jaw, Ash threw Pru a look that told her he had everything under control before turning back to Winter. "You can rest assured I did not allow Miss Winter to see the contents of the book in question. I was, quite regretfully, reading it when I looked out the window and spied her falling in the snow. In my haste to reach her and offer aid, I must have left the book lying about. The fault is purely mine."

"Rawdon," Winter growled now, his voice taut with barely suppressed aggression.

"Yes, Mr. Winter?" he asked, knowing a sound drubbing was likely heading his way.

"Get the hell away from my sister. Right. Bloody. Now."

Yes, he supposed lingering beneath the fur with Pru in his arms, her back nestled against his chest, her backside pressed to his hip, was not helping matters. Or his cause, for that matter. But still, he had no wish for Pru's brother to see him in his smalls. And if he took the fur along with him to the hearth, that would mean leaving Pru clad in only her fine chemise. Which would also be indecent.

He cleared his throat. "Would you mind turning your back, Mr. Winter?"

Winter looked as if he were about to spew fire. But he turned his back. "You have until the count of fifteen to get your miserable arse out of here, Rawdon. Await me in the adjoining chamber whilst I speak with my sister."

"Do not leave me," Pru whispered, sending Ash an entreating glance.

"I heard that," Winter called over his shoulder, his voice like a lash. "One, two, three…"

"I am sorry, sweet," he murmured to her, knowing Winter would be true to his word. The man would think nothing of tossing him into the snow, even if he were bare-arsed. And whilst Ashley was strong and he could match up well against the larger, burlier man, he had no desire to test the matter.

After all, this dreadful conundrum still needed to end with Ash winning the hand of the woman he loved. The woman he had yet to convince to become his wife. But as long as he threw on his breeches before Devereaux Winter murdered him, hopefully he would have ample time to persuade her.

Though he hated to leave her side, he forced himself from beneath the fur and stalked across the room. He dashed to his breeches and hauled them on before hastily stuffing his shirt over his head. The last time he had dressed in such haste and without the aid of his valet had been when he had been leaving the bed of a married lady whose cuckolded husband had returned unexpectedly. Spending an hour beneath a creaking bed while an elderly, drunken baron attempted to plow his wife had not been the proudest moment of Ash's life. Nor had the resultant tiptoeing away with his boots in his hands whilst the bastard snored.

"Fifteen," Winter announced, dragging Ash from the murky well of his past. "Get out, Rawdon."

Ash could have argued the point, demanded Winter to speak to him as befit his station. But he chose not to press the man's mercy. Instead, he snatched up the remainder of his garments, along with his boots, and offered an awkward bow before withdrawing from the chamber.

He hoped to God this would be the last time he ever left a chamber in dishabille, clutching his boots.

TO SAY HER brother was outraged would be akin to calling London a quaint little village.

The door had scarcely slammed on Lord Ashley's retreating form—and even cravenly exiting a chamber, he was still ridiculously handsome—when Dev began bellowing at her. Pru winced, wishing she could disappear into the settee. But she was a captive audience, as she was wearing only her chemise beneath the fur, and her beloved, overly protective brother was before her, insistent upon berating her for her lapse in judgment.

"—putting your future in grave danger, along with that of your sister who has yet to be spoken for," he was saying. "To say nothing of your sisters who are betrothed and are looking to find the path of acceptance in this damnable society! And you, of all our sisters, Pru. You have always been the rational sister. I can scarcely believe you would be the victim of a heartless rakehell like Rawdon. Did he force himself upon you? Do not fear telling me the truth, my dear. I will gut him like a fish if he did."

Oh, dear.

This was progressing rather worse than she had feared, after she had been jolted from the sweetest dreams she had ever had to Dev's scowling countenance.

"Lord Ashley did not force me," she said. "Please do calm down, Dev. As I told you, Lord Ashley was a gentleman. He did nothing untoward."

Except kiss her senseless, half disrobe her, and ask her to marry him.

But then he had come to her rescue, carried her through the storm, tended to her, warmed her, and held her in his arms as he asked her about the foundling hospital. And he had not pressed her for anything more. Nor had he attempted to seduce her. As time had worn on and they had chatted in the delicious warmth of the flames, she had reached a point where she had realized she would not have denied him if he had done so.

But he had not, and she did not want her brother to mistake the scene he had walked in on any more than he already had. Nor did she want to be forced into marrying Lord Ashley, she reminded herself.

"He did everything untoward," Dev bit out. "Instead of bringing you here, leaving you properly clothed, and stoking the fire before running back to Abingdon House for aid, the two of you somehow ended up bereft of your garments—"

"My garments were wet," she interrupted, "and I was freezing. Lord Ashley helped me out of them after I had taken a fall."

"I do not want to know what happened," her brother told her, pressing his fingers to his temples and rubbing, as if his head ached. "All I want to know is how much damage I will have to inflict upon him."

"None," she said, horrified at the prospect of Dev and Lord Ashley facing each other like a pair of prize fighters. "He helped me, you blockhead."

The moment the insult left her lips, she wished she could recall it.

Her brother's ears went red, so hot was his fury. "Would you care to insult me again, Prudence Winter?"

"No," she said. "I am sorry, Dev, but you are being rather unreasonable about all this."

"*Unreasonable?*" he repeated in a thunderous voice, his jaws clenching. "Pru, you were unclothed, alone, with Lord Ashley Rawdon, a man whose reputation is so wicked, I cannot even repeat some of the particulars in your presence. The two of you were witnessed here together by the footman who came to stoke the fire, who thankfully sought me before someone else could happen upon you."

Relief washed over her. It was a footman who had discovered them. Not another houseguest. Not a forbidding member of the aristocracy, who held to their tenets and rules.

"Then I am not truly compromised," she said, which was the first thought that arose in her mind.

"Yes, you are." Dev raked his fingers through his hair, leaving it standing on end. "There is no hope for it, Pru. You will have to marry Lord Ashley."

"I will not," she denied, clutching the fur more firmly around her. "If you are the only one who knows—"

"Along with the footman and whomever he chooses to tell," her brother interjected. "I do not know what I was thinking when my darling wife proposed we hold a Christmas country house party. I should have told her we would do nothing of the sort. Instead, I agreed like the lovesick puppy I am and now, all my sisters have taken leave of their senses. All save the very last sister I would have ever supposed would be the most rational and responsible."

Pru winced. Christabella was the wildest of their sisters. The most unflinchingly romantic. A true hellion. And yet, she was somehow the only sister who had not thus far been on the edge of finding herself embroiled in scandal.

Except…

Pru thought once more of the night she had run across Christabella, breathless and mussed in the halls, just after the Duke of Coventry had made his appearance in the west wing.

"Have you nothing to say for yourself?" her brother demanded.

She did not suppose she ought to ruin his delusion by informing him that the only sister he supposed was being rational and responsible was also doing nothing of the sort. Let him discover that when the time came.

"I am afraid I do not see the problem," she dared to say. "You wanted your sisters to find husbands. Bea, Eugie, and Grace have done so and are quite happy. Moreover, if Lord Ashley were indeed such a scoundrel, why would you have invited him here at all?"

"Because my wife wanted to invite the Duke of Coventry, and his scapegrace rakehell of a brother insisted upon accompanying him," Dev bit out. "That does not mean I intended for any of my sisters—least of all you—to marry the rogue."

Her brother's opinion of Lord Ashley only added to her misgiving. Part of him was outraged by their lapse in propriety, that much she knew. But his continued insistence about the unacceptable quality of Lord Ashley's reputation gave her pause.

"What has he done that is so horrid?" she demanded to know.

"I do not dare speak it aloud to my innocent sister," Dev

said, "though, if he was showing you that scandalous book—"

"Do forget about the book," she snapped, for it was her turn to interrupt this time. "Tell me about his reputation. If this is the man you will force me to wed, I deserve to know, do I not?"

Her brother had the grace to look shamefaced then. "You have forced yourself into marrying him with your reckless actions and your foolishness, Pru. I would never force you into anything."

"And yet you are standing before me, telling me I must marry him." The thought left her cold, for she had never imagined having no choice in her future. No say. That was the way of it for most women, but she was a Winter. She would possess a fortune in her own right.

"You are the reason you must marry him, Pru," Dev said pointedly.

"You do not even know if he is willing to marry me," she said.

"He will be," her brother vowed grimly.

She shuddered against the thought of Dev attempting to force Lord Ashley into marrying her. But of course, she already knew Lord Ashley was willing since he had proposed. The problem was, she did not know if he wanted to marry her for her share of the Winter fortune or for a different reason. And she still did not want to marry at all.

Or did she?

"Dev," she entreated, "please do not force us into a marriage. If his reputation is so horrid, you refuse to speak of it with me, surely you do not want to see me bound to him for the rest of my life. Do you?"

Dev looked more grim and determined than she had ever seen him before. His expression was harsh. Unyielding.

"You are marrying him, Pru. Your betrothal will be announced today, and that is the very best I can do for you at this point." He paused, his nostrils flaring. "The damage has already been done. There is nothing left for us now but to ameliorate it however we are able. Now kindly dress yourself and await me whilst I have a discussion with your future husband."

"No," she cried out, leaping to her feet, holding the fur against her as if it were a shield. "You cannot mean to do this, Dev."

"I can," he told her, and for a moment, there was a hint of the brother she loved in his countenance and his voice before it disappeared. "And I must."

Without waiting for her to respond, he turned and quit the chamber.

Chapter Ten

$\mathcal{A}$SH FOUND HIS brother in his chamber, dressing for dinner.

Following his uncomfortable interview with Devereaux Winter—which somehow, remarkably, had not led to blows—Gill was the one person he needed to see more than any other. His betrothal to Pru was to be announced this evening at dinner, and Ash felt like the world's greatest scoundrel for stealing the lady his brother had wanted to make his duchess. It was justified, for he loved her. But he also loved his brother.

Gill took one look at Ash, and an unspoken understanding passed between them.

"That is all, Martin," his brother dismissed his valet.

The servant quietly took his leave. Ash waited for the door to click closed before taking a deep breath and beginning his confession. And apology.

"I am in love with Pru," he said baldly.

Simultaneously, Gill said, "You have fallen in love with Miss Prudence Winter."

Ash's brows slammed together, for this was not what he had expected.

Not at all.

Not even close.

But then, his brother did have a propensity to surprise

him when he least expected it. Gill was also frightfully observant. Deuced insightful. Not being overly talkative gave him plentiful opportunity to watch everyone around him.

"How did you know?" he asked.

"You are my brother," Gill told him, as if that simple statement was explanation enough.

Another spear of guilt stabbed him. "How long have you known?"

"Since our arrival here." Gill faced him, unsmiling, and tied a simple knot in his cravat himself.

"Since our arrival," Ash repeated, his mind working to make sense of the revelation. "But what of the wager? You told me you wanted to make Pru your duchess."

"I told you I wanted to find my duchess here, and that I was willing to accept your aid," Gill countered. "We both know I am as useless as a ham when it comes to the fairer sex. You, however, were the one who suggested Miss Prudence."

"I was not," Ash denied. Gill had been the one to say Ash should begin with the eldest Winter. He was sure of it.

"You could not stop staring at her from the moment you first saw her," Gill said. "I had hoped the two of you might suit. You simply needed the proper motivation. A wager seemed just the thing."

"The devil." Ash was not certain if he should be insulted, outraged, or pleased. "You mean to tell me that this whole time, whilst I thought I was helping you to find a bride, *you*, my virginal, saintly brother, were actually helping *me* to acquire a bride?"

Gill smiled at last.

Actually, he grinned, the blighter.

"Yes."

"Confound it, Gill." He settled upon outrage for the moment. "Have you any idea how guilty I felt this last fortnight, believing I was lusting over the woman you wanted to make your duchess?"

"You ought to have done," his brother said, not even a modicum of contrition in his voice. "And if you had indeed been lusting after the woman I want to make my duchess, I would have planted you a facer."

That gave Ash pause. "The woman you want to make your duchess? Are you saying there *is* someone else you want to wed in attendance at this house party?"

"There may be," Gill said.

"Not the hellion," Ash said, his ire replaced by misgiving. Two more disparate souls could not possibly exist than his quiet, reserved brother and the flame-haired hoyden.

Gill finished tying his cravat. "I have no notion of whom you are speaking. I do trust, however, that you would not refer to your future wife's sister in such terms."

"Who said I am marrying Pru?" Ash asked.

"You," said his brother. "You have never once professed your love for a female to me. And from what I gather, the number of females with whom you have been on intimate terms is legion."

His ears went hot. The reminder of his past nettled him. He wished he could be pure and true and every bit as good as Pru was. He wished he had been virginal and virtuous, that he had spent the last few years of his life dedicated to awaiting the appearance of the woman he loved in his life instead of devoting himself to bedding an endless string of women.

But he could not change the past. He could not undo what had already been done. All he could do was his damnedest to make certain he spent the rest of his life with the woman he loved, doing his utmost to make her happy.

"I am not proud of the manner in which I have lived my life," he admitted to his brother, though the acknowledgment aggrieved him. "I have spent years chasing nothing but pleasure, telling myself it was what led to happiness. But I have discovered, quite belatedly, just how wrong I was. I do not deserve Pru, that much is certain. But I want to marry her."

"I am glad you have finally seen what has been plain enough to me," said his elder brother. "When will the betrothal be announced?"

"This evening," he said.

His brother's brows rose. "Remarkably quick of you, Ash."

"Yes, well." Ash attempted to tug at his own cravat, which had suddenly become damned restrictive. But then he realized he had not been able to don it in the wake of his ignominious discovery. The tightness in his throat was a manifestation of his own shame and nothing else. "I may have compromised Pru."

"You *may have* compromised her, or you *did*?" Gill demanded.

"I did." He grimaced. "It was unintentional, I swear it, and nothing untoward occurred. Well, actually, it did, but that was before we were discovered."

"Nothing you are saying is reassuring me," Gill said baldly.

Right. Ash could not blame his brother, for he was not wrong.

"It is...complicated. Suffice it to say, the lady took a fall in the snow, and I was left with no recourse but to help her disrobe so her garments would dry," he explained.

That, too, sounded quite nefarious. Even to his own jaded ears.

Gill's mouth flattened into a grim line. "Ash. Tell me you did not seduce her."

"I did not seduce her." He paused, raking a hand through his hair. "That is the truth. At least, not in the moment when we were discovered. But never mind that. We were in the false ruins, and my garments were quite sodden as well. I had no recourse but to join her beneath the fur, and then we—"

"Bloody hell, Ash!" Gill burst out. "Did you have to tup the sister of the woman I want to make my wife? Could you not have waited until the damned wedding night?"

"We fell asleep," Ash finished, indignant. Until the remainder of his brother's words hit him. "The woman you want to make your wife? You *do* want to marry the hellion."

"She is not a hellion," Gill snapped.

Laughter rose within Ash, out of nowhere. Ridiculous, mad laughter. He could not stay it, and it rang forth, deep and uncontrollable. He laughed until tears gathered in his eyes, and he wiped them with a handkerchief.

"What a pair we are," he said at last when he could catch his breath. "Perhaps I was right when I said there is something in the food here. A poison that rots men's minds and makes them more susceptible to matchmaking."

It was a statement he had made during the course of the house party, in passing, to the Earl of Hertford, Viscount Aylesford, and Gill. But now, it returned to him once more.

"The poison is love," his brother told him, his expression mournful.

"But is love a poison, or is it a cure?" Ash could not help but to ask, stroking his jaw as he contemplated the question himself. "It seems one could argue either way."

"One could, indeed," Gill said.

They were silent for a moment, unspoken acknowledgment passing between them.

"Let us hope it is a cure," Ash decided.

For he had to believe that, or all was lost. Just as he had to believe he could convince Pru to become his bride. For although Mr. Devereaux Winter had informed him in succinct, precise—not to mention threatening—terms, that he must marry Pru, the lady herself had already denied him. And he wanted to win her hand every bit as much as he wanted to win her heart.

He would not rest until both were his.

HER BETROTHAL HAD been announced.

Dev had done what he had promised he would do. And Lord Ashley, it seemed, was willing to marry her. Not that she would know, because from the moment he had bolted from beneath the fur they had shared earlier that day, she had not even had the opportunity to speak with him alone. All eyes had been upon them at dinner during the announcement, and when the ladies of the company had withdrawn, she had been so aggrieved that she had excused herself and sought her bed early.

Not the actions of a happy future bride, it was certain. But she did not care. Having her life decided for her by others was certainly the sorry fate most ladies found themselves in. It was not, however, the fate she had anticipated for herself. Particularly since Dev had allowed each of her other sisters to agree to their betrothals.

Oh, she knew he was being protective—of her, and of her other sisters as well, especially Christabella, who had yet to become betrothed. Still, she was angry with him. Angry with herself as well. And, most importantly, angry with Lord Ashley, the wickedly handsome, utterly charming, terribly tempting rakehell she was now betrothed to wed.

To that end, she was lying in the dark, staring at the

ceiling, rolling this way and that, pummeling her pillow, and attempting to get more comfortable. But no matter how many times she rolled to her left side from her right, and regardless of how much fluffing of her pillow she performed, and despite the lateness of the hour and the blackness of the night, Pru still could not sleep. How could she, when her entire future had been decided for her with nary a word of her own acceptance? When she had no inkling of where she stood with Lord Ashley?

He was a rogue, she reminded herself for at least the hundredth time that evening alone. A scoundrel. Not to be trusted. It was entirely possible he had planned for them to be caught. That he had compromised her intentionally. And if he had...

Suddenly, the door to her chamber opened. An all-too-familiar voice cut through the stillness of the night. "Pru?"

She jolted upright in bed, clutching the bedclothes to her. "Lord Ashley?"

"You were not expecting anyone else, I hope," he murmured, the door clicking shut behind him. "Do you not suppose you might call me Ash by now?"

"I was not expecting anyone." She kept her voice tart. Pointed.

He was not welcome here, she told herself, and she must remain firm on that. Moreover, calling him Ash still felt far too intimate. And though they had shared a great deal with each other earlier today, so much uncertainty still swirled within her. His footsteps creaked across the floor. Until the unmistakable sound of his foot connecting with a piece of furniture echoed through the chamber.

"Blast," he muttered.

She bit her lip. "Are you injured, my lord?"

"Desperately," he said, but his voice was nearer now than

before, and followed by the unmistakable depression of her bed. "I fear I may lose the toe."

"You are bamming me," she accused without heat, a smile rising to her lips she could not seem to stifle.

"Your lack of faith in my integrity wounds," he drawled.

"What are you doing in my bedchamber?" she demanded next. "Have you not already caused enough scandal for me today?"

He moved closer on the bed, making it dip more. "As I doubt I can compromise you any further than I already have, I considered the risk of coming here to you worth the reward."

She scooted nearer to the opposite edge of her bed, putting some necessary distance between them once more. If he was too near, she would lose her ability to resist him. It happened every time.

"You still have not explained why you are here, disrupting my slumber." Not that she had been sleeping, but he need not know that.

He patted the bedclothes. "Devil take it, where are you, Pru? And how big is this cursed bed?"

"Go away, Lord Ashley," she ordered, desperate for him to go.

If he touched her, she would melt like snow beneath the heat of a blazing summer sun. The mere thought of the pleasure he had given her earlier that day was enough to make her feel needy and achy, from the points of her hardened nipples to the throbbing flesh between her thighs.

His hand was patting still. In the murky darkness, the curtains drawn tightly. Suddenly, it settled upon her breast, his fingers instantly cupping her. "There you are," he said, his voice thick.

Her heart beat faster, but she shooed his hand away. "Have you come here to grope me, my lord?"

"I came to speak with you, which I would have done earlier in the drawing room had you not hidden yourself away," he returned. "I found your breast quite unintentional-ly."

She was willing to wager a rakehell like him could find her breast in the darkest, most moonless of nights with ease. "As unintentionally as you found your way into my chamber and spent the last fortnight following me about."

He sighed. "As we have already established, the following was intentional. For a good cause, or so I believed at the time. It quickly became a personal cause rather than the original intention."

The bedclothes moved then, and a draft of cool air swept over her, cutting through her night rail. Suddenly, a large, undeniably male body scooted alongside hers. The scoundrel had joined her in bed. Entirely uninvited. Thoroughly improperly.

She ought to evict him at once.

And yet, finding the tart words she wanted took her some time. She could not seem to speak them. Because there was something about Lord Ashley Rawdon pressed against her, in her bed, that felt so very right. Every bit as right as kissing him had.

He discovered her hand, tangling his fingers through hers. And that was when she located her voice at last. But still, she did not extricate her hand from his grasp. Rather, she gave his long fingers a squeeze. Because this, too, felt right.

"What are you doing here, Lord Ashley?" she asked quiet-ly, lest she alert anyone beyond her chamber to his presence.

One scandal a day was enough, thank you very much.

"Will you not call me Ash from now on?" he returned, raising her hand to his lips for a kiss. "It would please me greatly."

Oh, how easily he broke through her walls.

He smelled of sunshine and decadent man. Everything delicious. Everything so wonderfully, wickedly him.

"Ash," she relented at last. "You cannot linger here in my bedchamber, in my bed. It is horribly improper."

"I was supposed to have learned the rules of proper courtship from you, but you never completed your duty," he said. "Therefore, you can hardly fault me for my ignorance. I am courting you the only way I know how."

In bed. That part, she believed. She did not particularly care for the jealousy accompanying such thoughts, however.

"You are courting me?" she repeated. The man was a rake. Utterly mad.

"I am attempting to do so, yes," he said in his low, delicious baritone.

The one that never failed to send thrills skittering through her.

"Even a rake like you has to know that this is not the proper form of courting." She pursed her lips, studying him through the darkness. She could see the outline of his handsome face—the strong jaw, the blade of his nose, the proud cheekbones, the sensual mouth. Just enough to make her ache for him.

She remembered, all too well, the sensation of his fingers between her thighs. His mouth on her breasts. Concentrating upon her irritation with him was growing more impossible by the moment. He smelled so good. He felt so good. Next to him felt, oddly, like the only place she ever wanted to be.

"I wanted to be certain you wish to marry me," he said then, his tone tender.

Hesitant, too. As if he were afraid of her answer.

For the first time, his polished rake's veneer had slipped.

"You could have asked me tomorrow," she pointed out.

"I could not bear to go another sleep without knowing."

There was a rawness to his voice, to his words. A compelling note of honesty.

"And why should you care, either way?" she forced herself to demand, reminding herself she could not be sure of him, that she did not dare. "You have what you wanted: me as your bride. Why should you concern yourself with whether or not I am willing?"

"Because I want you to be happy, Pru." He gave her fingers a squeeze and rolled to face her, lying on his side and propping his chin in his other hand. "I want to marry you, but only if you want to marry me in return."

But she did not want to marry him. She wanted her freedom. Her foundling hospital. She did not want to be tied to a handsome rake she could not trust, even if he made her weak and wanting.

"I am afraid my opinion in the matter holds little weight when I have been so thoroughly ruined and my brother is all but forcing me into wedding you." She could not expunge the bitterness from her voice. "We were unclothed together beneath a shared fur. The evidence against us is most damning."

"To the devil with the evidence, Pru," he said, more serious than she had ever heard him. "Regardless of how much I long to have you as my wife, I cannot be content with your unhappiness."

Would she be unhappy as his wife?

What a foreign notion, becoming this gorgeous, sleek, seductive man's bride. When she had thought of her future before she had met him, she had imagined only the foundling hospital she wanted to build. Could she still have that future, but with him? And more importantly, could she trust him?

"So tell me, Pru, what would make you happy?" he prodded into the silence that had descended between them.

"My own foundling hospital." That part of her answer was simple. Easy. The rest? Not so much.

"What if we were to build it together?" he asked then, giving her fingers another squeeze.

"Build a foundling hospital with you," she repeated, in a daze at the notion. He had her dizzied all over again from his nearness, from his words, from the warm buzz within her that was growing stronger, hotter, louder, deeper.

"Do not sound so dubious at the notion, Pru." He raised their linked hands to his lips for another kiss. "It is true that I am no saint. But I want to be better for you."

"Your reputation is so wicked my brother would not even dare to repeat it aloud to me," she said, reminded of his past.

Reminded he was a rakehell. A handsome scoundrel. A man accustomed to getting whatever he wanted. A man who was not to be trusted, regardless of the sweet temptation of his kisses and touches.

"I cannot change my past, but I can promise to be the best husband I can possibly be to you," he told her. "I am not the same man I once was, though I was a hellion, and there is no denying it."

She wished suddenly that it was not so dark in her chamber, for she wanted to see his face. Look into his eyes. But even in the absence of light, she swore she could hear the sincerity in his voice, and it resonated deep within her, landing inside her heart.

Where it planted a tiny seed.

Hope.

And something stronger, too, but she refused to think it could possibly be...

Of course it could not be *that*. She could not even think the word. Would not think it. Because she could not feel it.

Not for this man, this wicked rake.

The man kissing her hand, then each one of her fingers as if she were the most precious gift ever bestowed upon him. "Say something, sweet."

"Why do you want to marry me?" she asked him then. "Truly?"

"Because I love you, Pru," he said, shocking her to her core. "Could you not already tell? I have been chasing you, it is true, all over this house party as you accused me. But not like a lost puppy. Rather, a lovesick one. I think I fell in love with you the moment I first saw you."

"You…love me." The words felt foreign and unfamiliar on her tongue. Impossible, too. "But how can that be?"

"It can be, Pru Winter," he said, releasing her hand to caress her cheek, "because you are the most beautiful woman I have ever seen, from the inside out. Your heart is pure and true. You are intelligent and strong, fierce and loyal, protective of your sisters, daring and sweet and bold. You are everything I could want in my wife. The way you speak of the children at the foundling hospital—your love for them is plain, and I admire you for that, for loving those who need it most, for offering up your heart so selflessly. And I find myself hoping that one day, somehow, you may find space enough in your saint's heart for a sinner like me."

The seed he had planted sprouted. And it grew. She knew the name for the feeling, for the rush inside her chest, that strange sensation, as if she were glowing from within. As if she were light as air and yet heavy as an anvil, all at once.

That feeling was *love*.

Indescribable, really. Transforming, absolutely. Incredible and terrifying all at once.

She was in love with Lord Ashley Rawdon.

With *Ash*.

And he was in love with her.

"Pru, sweet," he rasped, his voice strained. His thumb

continued its slow, steady exploration of her cheek. "Say something. Preferably that you will wed me and put me out of my eternal misery."

"Ash," she said, trying his name out once more, saying it aloud.

Though it was not the first time, it felt different now. Like a promise.

"That is my name," he agreed wryly.

It was her turn to reach through the inkiness of the night, to frame his face in her hands. She cupped his jaw, absorbing his resilient warmth, the wonderful prickle of his whiskers. "Did you mean what you said about building a foundling hospital with me?"

"Of course. I want to meet all the children at the hospital your brother funds," he told her. "We can go there together. And we will build another, one even bigger and better. We will give second chances to those who would otherwise be lost."

There was an edge underscoring his words, and Pru understood for the first time that though he was a handsome rake, and he had charmed his way through the ladies of London, Ash related to those children who had been left behind. The children no one loved. Perhaps, in a sense, he saw some of himself in them.

"Nothing would make me happier," she told him softly. "I will be your wife."

"Thank Christ," he muttered, and then his lips were on hers.

The kiss was hot and dark and passionate, a possession. She rolled onto her side as well, pressing her body to his. The thick ridge of his manhood prodded her belly. She knew precisely what it was thanks to *The Tale of Love*. And because she had felt it before. Their tongues met as a frenzied rush of need swept over her. An ache only he could answer.

There was one more thing she wanted to say, however.

With great reluctance, she broke the kiss, tipping her head back to meet his gaze through the shadows. "There is something I need to tell you, Ash."

"Whatever it is, tell me quickly so I can commence ravishing you," he said, his voice thick.

She had to stave off a soaring tide of desire. Because these words were important. They were necessary. She wanted to get this right. But in the end, she simply blurted it out.

"I love you."

There. She had spoken them, and they seemed to echo in the night. He stilled, his hands on her tightening wherever they held her.

"Do you mean it?" he asked, sounding uncertain.

It was the last reaction she expected from a man like him, and it pushed her over the edge. Made her more certain, even, than she had been before, of him, of herself, of their love. Of what a future with him could be like. Would be like, if she but gave it and Ash the chance.

"Of course I do," she told him. "I love you, Ash. I love every gloriously improper part of you."

"But my past, Pru," he protested, "I cannot change it. I cannot alter who I once was."

"I know that." She paused, searching for the right words, the way to allay his fears. "I do not want you to change. I want you exactly as you are, who you are. Because you are the man I fell in love with. The wicked rake, the protective brother, the teasing scoundrel, the man who chased me through sleet and snow and carried me in his arms to take me to where I would be dry and warm, the man who kisses me so sweetly…"

"I want to kiss you again now," he warned her, his hands on her waist, drawing her even nearer. His nose brushed hers. "I cannot wait another bloody second."

"Then don't," she said.

Chapter Eleven

*P*RU DID NOT have to tell him twice.

His lips were on hers before she even finished the last word of her sentence. Because he was ravenous for her. So hungry. Their mouths moved as one, open and voracious. Tongues mated. Teeth nipped. His cock was harder than it had ever been, buried into the softness of her belly when all he wanted to do was sink it inside her.

He could not, of course.

Nor would he.

There would be a wedding first. He was determined not to take Pru's maidenhead until she was truly his wife. But tonight was a celebration of love, of each other. He could still not believe, even as her delectable body pressed into his and the sweet summery scent of her filled his senses, that she had agreed to be his. That she loved him too.

It was almost too good to be real.

But the desire roaring through him, demanding to be answered, proved he was not imagining this. He would go as far as he dared before returning to his chamber. And by the morning light, he would convince Devereaux Winter to allow him to marry Pru with as much haste as possible. Because he wanted to begin the rest of his life right bloody now.

He would start here, with venerating the woman he loved in the best way he knew how, by showing her how much he loved her. Pru wore only a night rail, but he needed it gone. He wanted there to be no barrier between him and her glorious body for the first time. Though he had more than his fair share of lovers in his past, he had never been in love with them.

Slowly, he raised her hem, all the way to her waist. Meanwhile, his lips never left hers. She tasted of the sweetness of the syllabub they had enjoyed for dessert. He wanted to devour her. Everything with Pru felt new and alive and fresh in a way he could not have conceived. Gratitude swept over him, for this beautiful woman in his life, for her generous heart. For the love she gave so freely and selflessly.

But he reminded himself he could not simply tear the nightdress from his beloved tyro. No, indeed. He would have to proceed slowly, exercising caution and grace. With great reluctance, he tore his lips from hers, staring down into her beautiful face.

"Pru," he rasped. "I need to feel you. I promise you, I will not take things too far. But if I do not have you naked in the next five seconds, I shall die."

It was not an exaggeration.

His heart was pounding, and all the blood in his body had surged to his rigid cock.

He was desperate to feel her soft, silken curves without a barrier, from head to toe.

She saved him from imminent demise, however, by grasping the hem he had raised and hauling the night rail over her head herself. There was a flutter of fabric dropping to the floor, and then in the low light of the moon seeping through the window dressings, he spied the creamy swells of her breasts.

Ash was on her, kissing her again, weighing her breasts in his palms. Her nipples were already hard, the buds a sensual invitation he could not resist. He kissed his way down her throat and then latched on to one, sucking greedily.

She moaned, her fingers sliding into his hair, tightening.

He would never tire of how deliciously uninhibited she was. Thank the Lord she was a sensual creature. Thank the Lord she was *his*. And she loved him. That knowledge was still too new. Still too good to be true.

Ash sucked the peak of her other breast into his mouth next, then flicked his tongue over it before releasing it. Puckering his lips, he blew cool air over the taut bud. She made a sound, part purr, part growl. And it spurred him on. He caught her nipple in his teeth and tugged.

"Harder," she said.

Nay. Surely he had misheard her. He released her nipple with a lusty, wet pop.

"Pardon?"

"Do it again," she ordered him, guiding him back to her breast. "Harder this time."

Christ. The desire thundering through him could not be contained. There was nothing more carnal and delicious than Pru taking command of her own pleasure. He took her nipple in his teeth and gently nipped.

Her fingers tugged his hair, and the mixture of painful pleasure had him on edge. If he did not soon unbutton the fall of his breeches, he would spend within them like a callow youth.

"Not enough," she whispered. "Bite it."

Fucking hell.

This woman would be the death of him. Even so, it would be the most pleasurable death imaginable. "Your servant, Miss Winter."

He bit.

She jerked, body bowing from the bed. Her mound

arched into his raging cockstand. The air fled his lungs, and a white-hot burst of need licked down his spine, drawing his ballocks tight.

"Oh, Ash." Her passion-laden sigh was the ultimate aphrodisiac. "More, please."

Strike that. The words *more, please* from her berry-pink lips was.

It was all he wanted to hear. Every damned day and night. That and *I love you.*

He caught her hard nipple in his teeth once again, nipping with greater force before he sucked, using his tongue to soothe the sting. He released her then and kissed the generous swell of her breast.

"Tell me what you want me to do," he said, kissing a path down her abdomen. Intent upon setting his tongue to her at last.

"Use your mouth…"

Her husky directive trailed off as he kissed her belly button and then dipped his tongue into the sensitive little pit. Her hips shot off the bed in response.

"Oh," she said.

"Mmm," he responded. And then he continued his quest.

He kissed his way to her sex. His hands were on her thighs now, caressing, guiding them apart. He settled between them. How he wished for a lit brace of candles in this moment. He wanted to see the exact shade of pink, the erotic glistening of her juices upon her cunny. All of it, and all of her, he wanted to see in explicit detail.

But he would have to wait for another night.

Tonight, he would have to rely upon his other senses. He flattened his palms against the softness of her inner thighs, spreading them wide. The heat from her core, along with the sweet, musky scent of her, was enough to spur him on.

"Pru, sweet Pru," he said. "I want to eat you."

It was a warning. A statement. His hunger for her knew no end. But if he had supposed he would shock her, he was wrong.

"Do it," she said.

He did not waste another second. Ash's face was between her thighs, his tongue flicking over her pearl. His hands slid from her inner thighs to her rump, where he cupped her. His hands were filled with soft, supple, warm bottom. He thought about licking her cunny all the way to that forbidden, puckered hole, licking her there. Then he thought about all there was to show her, all the ways he could give her pleasure.

Ash inhaled deeply, and it was the decadent scent of Pru. The heart of her. Woman and musk, earthy yet sweet. He wanted to lick her until she spent, and then he wanted to start licking her all over again. He could not get enough of her.

He sucked her slick pearl into his mouth.

She moaned.

Her hips rotated, then thrust.

She was unafraid of her sensual nature, fully embracing it, thoroughly Pru. And he loved every moment of it. Just as he loved *her*.

He flicked his tongue up her slit, and then he sank between her folds, finding her opening. He flicked his tongue against her, shallowly at first. But then, he could not resist thrusting inside. Possessing her as he had longed to do since he had first met her gaze from across a crowded ballroom.

How long ago it seemed now.

He licked into her, sinking his tongue as far as it would go. Her channel tightened on him, and she was making all sorts of wondrous sounds. Sounds of surrender. He flicked his tongue over her pearl once more. Alternating between sucking and lashing, he set himself to the task. When she stiffened

145

beneath him, thrusting her cunny into his face, he almost spent then and there. She was close. So close to coming undone. And undone was precisely the way he wanted her. He wanted to make her come so hard, she saw stars.

So hard, her chest hurt.

So hard, she would never come again without comparing it to this time, to this spend. To her first with a man's lips and tongue upon her. To his mouth on her cunny, her essence on his tongue, his hands on her arse, cupping her, raising her to his mouth.

Damn it to hell, he could not get enough. He lapped at her. Sucked her. Licked her. Fucked her with his mouth, his tongue. And still, it was not enough. She was writhing beneath him, on the edge. At last, he recalled her words, what she had said when he had been sucking on her nipple earlier. *Harder. Bite it.* She was a tigress, his Pru.

Ash returned to her clitoris, raking it between his teeth. One subtle tug was all he required to send her careening into madness. She quaked beneath him, writhing, her hips moving, her hands in his hair, urging him on.

Words and speech were beyond him now. She was everything, urging him on.

Pru moaned. "Oh, Ash."

He would happily pleasure her forever. She spent in a torrent, her juices flooding his tongue, and he licked them up, swallowed them down. His spoils. All his, for the taking. But if he lingered a second more, he would never want to go, could not force himself to leave her side and her bed as he must.

Reluctantly, he kissed a path up her body, all the way to her forehead. He planted the last just over her left brow. How he hated to put an end to this, but he knew he must, before he reached the point of no return.

"Thank you, sweet," he murmured. "I will go to bed with the memory of you."

"To the devil with the memory of me," she said, gripping his biceps and holding him fast when he would have left her bed. "I am here now, Ash."

Here was an invitation he could not accept. She was delirious from her climax. She did not know what she was saying. As the one with more experience, he would have to prevail.

"Of course you are," he agreed, softly, "but I cannot take this any further, sweet. Not until we are wed."

No matter the temptation she presented, naked and warm, all luscious curves and silken seduction. Though he was still clad in breeches, shirt, and cravat, his body was aligned to hers, and she was ready for the taking. Not that he would do it. He should not, he knew. It would he scandalous. Disreputable. Dishonorable.

Delicious.

Fuck.

He had precious little resistance when it came to the woman he loved.

"I want you," she said, and there was no doubt as to what she meant.

She wanted his cock. Inside her.

Bloody hell, he was marrying a minx.

And he could not be more pleased.

PRU WAS THE eldest of her sisters.

She had always been the voice of reason.

But she did not feel reasonable, wise, or particularly prudent in this moment. No, indeed. All she felt was the aching need for the man she loved.

"We should wait until we are married," he told her tenderly, kissing her cheek. "I have already ruined you thoroughly enough."

"Yes, you have," she agreed, releasing his arms to pluck at the knot in his cravat. "You may as well finish what you have started."

"Pru." Her name was a groan.

But he did not make a move to leave. Instead, he kissed her ear. The knot she had been working upon gave way, and she tugged it free, before tossing it into the darkness. Where it landed, she did not care. Then, her fingers settled upon the buttons of his shirt. She wanted his bare chest. Nothing but his skin.

Together, they hauled the shirt over his head. Her fingers explored him. Warm, solid male flesh. Rigid slabs of taut muscle. A dusting of crisp masculine hair. His chest was strong, his belly lean. Touching him sent an arrow of heat to the still-throbbing flesh between her thighs.

"I should go now," he said.

"You should stay," she countered, making her way to the fall of his breeches.

He caught her hand, staying her. "If you take off my breeches, I am going to make love to you, Pru."

His words of warning sent a frisson of desire unfurling through her. "Good."

She slid her hand down the front of his soft breeches, gratified when he exhaled sharply and his hips jerked into her. His cock was thick and long, pressing into her palm. And warm, so very warm. Her core pulsed.

Reading *The Tale of Love* had given her all the forbidden knowledge she needed.

"Pru," he said again, his voice strained. He kissed her

throat. His hand moved over hers, molding her fingers around the shape of him.

"Mmm," she said appreciatively, rolling her body against his, beyond words.

She wanted to drown in the pleasure he was giving her. To be the wild and reckless Winter sister. Just this once. Because in his arms, in the darkness, their bodies pressed together, she felt fearless and powerful all at once.

"Damn it," he growled.

He released her hand, opening the fall of his breeches, then removing his body from hers long enough to tug them and his stockings free of his body. When he rejoined her, they were both naked in truth. He settled between her thighs, her legs opening instinctively to welcome him.

This man was made for her.

And she was made for him.

His mouth was on hers in a long, passionate kiss. She tasted herself on his lips and tongue. It was shocking yet exciting. His tongue played with hers, and he rolled his hips, letting her feel all of him.

He broke the kiss. "You are sure, Pru?"

"I have never been more certain of anything," she assured him, breathless.

His fingers dipped into her folds, parting her, finding the most sensitive part. Sparks seemed to shoot from her there, dancing up and down her spine. She moved restlessly, seeking more.

He gave it to her, fitting the tip of his cock to her entrance. The sensation was new and strange. Tantalizing. And then, he moved. One slow thrust, and he was inside her. Stretching her. Filling her.

The breath left her. She clutched his shoulders, her fingers digging into his muscles.

He was still. "Does it hurt, love?"

"No." There was a twinge, a slight burn. "You feel wonderful."

He did. Ash inside her was perfection. His fingers were working their magic once more, flicking over her bud, making her senses sing. He moved again, sinking deeper inside her. The feeling was exquisite. One more pump of his hips, and he was seated all the way.

Their lips fused once more as he began a rhythm, slowly at first. In and out, heightening the already intense pleasure soaring inside her. She kissed him back, learning from him, moving her hips in time with his. The desire within her rose to a crescendo, wild and uncontrollable, until she could not last for another moment more.

She exploded. Her channel tightened on him as ecstasy burst inside her. Tiny white stars showered over her vision. She cried out into his mouth, and he swallowed it, still moving within her as bliss rolled from her core to all her limbs. Even her fingers and toes were tingling. She was alive, so very alive. Awash in him. Lost in him.

He tore his mouth from hers, then plunged deep. His body went stiff in her arms. On a series of shallow thrusts, he reached his pinnacle as well, emptying himself. The heady rush of his seed within her made Pru spend once more. Her body bowed from the bed as she arched against him on one final shudder of pure, carnal bliss.

They remained as they were, locked together, their breathing mutually ragged.

"My God, I love you, Pru," he said.

"I love you, too," she told him, happiness washing over her. She was sated, limp, blissful, and one with the rake who had stolen her heart.

"I am going to marry you as soon as I damned well can."

He kissed her cheek, then swept a tendril of hair from her face.

"You had better," she agreed, caressing his back. "For you have just truly ruined me, my lord."

But oh, how right being ruined felt.

"I fear I have once more violated the rules of proper courting," he told her, his voice teasing.

"I am glad you did," she said smiling back at him through the darkness, and then she tugged his head back down to hers, sealing their lips in another kiss.

Epilogue

$\mathcal{A}$SH HAD BEEN a husband for only three months, and he was already a father twice over.

His fatherhood was not, however, because of his inability to await the consummation of his marriage. Of which, of course, he had been guilty. And not just on the one occasion, either. There had been the initial night he had slipped into Pru's chamber, but after they had been forced to wait three weeks for the banns to be read, there had also been that time in the library, those two times in the west wing salon, a fifth indiscretion in the false ruins, not to mention that hasty coupling in the holly maze, which had been deuced cold but worth every second of freezing air on his ballocks…

Curse it, if he was not careful, Ash was going to be sporting a cockstand, which was decidedly *de trop* for a gentleman standing on the threshold of the nursery, admiring his lady wife as she rocked their twin daughters to sleep. Jane and Mary and been the newest additions to her brother's foundling hospital. Left behind by an overwhelmed young mother with no means of providing for two infants at once, the babes had been named by the hospital, and were about to be separated, sent to two different wet nurses.

When he and Pru had returned to London following their nuptials, the babes had stolen both their hearts, and neither of them wanted to see the sisters torn apart. Meanwhile, twins had been a daunting prospect for the already crowded foundling hospital. Ash and Pru's decision had been easy and swift. And over the last few weeks, Ash had come to discover an equally beloved role, alongside that of Pru's husband.

That of papa.

"How are our angels?" he asked softly.

Pru looked up at him, a tender smile of welcome on her lips. She held one babe in her left arm and one arm in her right, and he did not think he had ever seen a more wondrous sight than the three ladies he loved most, all together in the soft glow of the evening candlelight.

"They are sleeping at last, I do believe," she murmured *sotto voce*, so as not to wake the slumbering infants. "How is the new foundling hospital coming along?"

He had just arrived back home from his tour of the progress of the foundling hospital they were building alongside the existing building her brother patronized. Although Devereaux Winter had been more than generous with his fortune, and the hospital was large, clean, and well-run by a compassionate staff, there remained more babes in need of homes than space for them. Children were admitted on the basis of a balloted system. With the addition of a new building, Ash and Pru hoped no children would need to be turned away.

"Construction is almost complete," he reported to Pru. "I expect in the next sennight, we will be able to have the furnishings moved in and the staff you are selecting will be able to begin as well."

"Thank you for all the work you have done on behalf of the hospital and the children," she told him, love shining in her eyes.

"It gives me a purpose," he said easily, for it did.

Who could have guessed that Lord Ashley Rawdon, one

of the most scandalous rakes in London, would have found happiness in being a husband and father, and in surrounding himself with abandoned children? He had never supposed such joy was possible for him. But it was, all thanks to the goddess he had found quite unexpectedly one Oxfordshire Christmastide.

"Speaking of purpose," his wife said, raising a brow at him. "Would you take one of the girls and settle her in her crib for me?"

Ash was at her side in a trice, lifting Jane from Pru's arms. He held the precious little bundle to his chest. She was sleeping so soundly, she did not even stir. Love, profound and strong, hit him as he stared down at the sleeping face of his daughter.

"There is Papa's angel," he murmured softly, before kissing her brow.

He settled her in her crib with ease, then gave her bottom a soothing pat before drawing the blanket over her. She made a sigh of contentment and raised her tiny fist to her mouth, sucking on it in her sleep.

Pru settled Mary in the crib alongside her sister, then fussed with the blankets. Ash watched his wife with a mixture of pride and love. She was a wonderful mother, just as he had known she would be. He felt immeasurably blessed. Undeserving of the happiness in which he found himself, but appreciative of it. So very thankful for Pru and the family they had begun.

"There we are," his wife said gently, giving the blanket a final adjustment before turning toward him. "Since the girls should be soundly sleeping for the next little while, perhaps we might retire for just a bit. Supper will not be for another hour."

The hint of wicked suggestion in her voice was all he

needed to hear. "Lead the way, my love."

PRU HAD SCARCELY made it over the threshold of her chamber before her husband's hands were on her waist. She had news to share with him, but it could wait, because she was suddenly ravenous for him. He nuzzled her neck, planting a kiss there and inhaling deeply.

"You smell so damned good," he told her. "Every time I smell a flower, my cock gets hard."

She chuckled and reached back to thread her fingers through his soft, thick hair. "It is soap from my brother's factory."

He hummed his approval before tonguing the sensitive hollow behind her ear. "Do me a favor, love, and do not mention your brother when I am about to fuck you. It rather dampens the mood."

She laughed again. "You, sir, are a rogue."

"Unapologetically," he agreed, his hand gliding from her waist to her bottom, before giving her derriere a squeeze. "A rogue who cannot wait another minute to be inside his beautiful wife."

His words sent a furl of molten longing through her. "Then you should not wait."

Her voice was breathless with anticipation. Because she was every bit as eager for him as he was for her. She turned around in his arms, and then, they were kissing. Their lips met and held, tongues tangling as they began stripping each other of their garments. Her gown fell away. So, too, his coat and cravat. Their shoes were next, followed by her stays and petticoat, his waistcoat and shirt.

When every piece of fabric had been haphazardly strewn

across the Aubusson, they fell into the bed together. Ash tore his mouth from hers and positioned her on all fours, leaving her rump high in the air. It was a position they both loved, for it allowed him to drive deeply inside her.

His fingers slid through her folds, finding her pearl with effortless precision. "Damn, Pru. You are so wet for me."

Yes, she was.

He sank a finger inside her, and she gasped, her hips beginning to pump with an urgent need. "I want you," she told him, arching her back.

She was on full display for him, and she loved it.

She loved everything they did together.

Ash had taught her to embrace her sensuality. To revel in it. To never be ashamed of her wants or needs.

A second finger joined the first as he worked her clitoris with his thumb. But just when she was going to spend, he withdrew. She was about to protest when he pressed the head of his cock to her opening. She shifted restlessly, wanting his penetration.

He took his time, playing with her. His fingers slid along her folds, and she was so wet now that the sound of him playing with her echoed in the chamber. He slicked some of her dew higher, finding another place. One that also wanted his touch. Oh so slowly, he swirled his touch over her there, driving her wild.

Just when she thought she could bear no more of his sensual torture, he gave her what she wanted. He filled her in one thrust, sliding his thumb inside her at the same time. In and out he went, the rhythm building a sweet crescendo of flame inside her. He was filling her in the most delicious way, and she could not hold herself together for another second more.

She spent, crying out as a fierce climax erupted within

her.

The pleasure was so intense, she collapsed to the bed, her face pressed into the counterpane as an intense rush swept over her. Two more thrusts, and he was coming too, the hot spurt of his seed heightening her pleasure.

He fell to the bed at her side, breathing heavily, a wicked, sated grin on his lips. "That was an excellent welcome home, my love."

She found her tongue at last, lying there, admiring the golden god she had married. And that was when she remembered her news.

"There is something I must tell you, Ash," she said, still breathless from their lovemaking.

His brow furrowed. "What is it, sweet?"

The intensity of what they had just shared rendered it impossible for her to think of a proper way to relay the words. So she simply blurted it out.

"Our family is soon going to grow."

"Grow?" he asked, his gaze searching hers.

"Yes." She smiled at him. "I am going to have a babe."

"Bloody hell, woman," he growled, cupping her face. "Why did you not say so sooner?"

"I was being ravished by my husband," she pointed out wryly, studying him. "You are pleased?"

"Pleased?" The smile he gave her filled her heart. "I am thrilled. So damned happy."

"Good." She drew him to her for a kiss. "Jane and Mary will be happy to be big sisters as well, I should think."

"They will be quite pleased indeed," he agreed, his voice tender. "I love our family."

"And we love you," she said.

Pru had been wrong, she thought, when she had supposed a bargain with a rake would only lead her to trouble. Instead, her bargain with a rake had led her to love. And happiness.

He kissed her again, then rolled her onto her back.

Pleasure, too.

One could not forget that.

But then, her husband's lips were worshiping a path down her body, and all thoughts fled. Instead, she basked in the glory of the wicked bargain she had made with her rake. Because he was hers now, just as she was his.

Forever.

THE END

Dear Reader,

Thank you for reading *Wagered in Winter*! I hope you enjoyed this fifth book in my The Wicked Winters series and that Ash and Pru's story gave you a smile and a bit of swoon. I love my Winter family, and I thank you, the readers, for loving them too!

As always, please consider leaving an honest review of *Wagered in Winter*. Reviews are greatly appreciated! If you'd like to keep up to date with my latest releases and series news, sign up for my newsletter here or follow me on Amazon or BookBub. Join my reader's group on Facebook for bonus content, early excerpts, giveaways, and more.

If you'd like a preview of *Wild in Winter*, Book Six in The Wicked Winters, featuring the spirited Miss Christabella Winter and the mysterious Duke of Coventry, do read on.

Until next time,

Scarlett

Wild in Winter

BY
SCARLETT SCOTT

Gill, the Duke of Coventry, has never been the sort of gentleman who woos ladies with effortless ease. In fact, he's never even kissed a woman, let alone courted one. But as the new duke, he's in need of a wealthy bride to replenish his dwindling familial coffers. Preferably a sweet, calm bride who is equally reserved. A bride who is nothing at all like Miss Christabella Winter.

Christabella is looking for passion. She longs for forbidden kisses in hidden alcoves, for a dashing rake to sweep her off her feet. Therefore, her dratted infatuation with the shy Duke of Coventry makes no sense. Particularly since he cannot be bothered to speak to her in complete sentences.

When she inadvertently learns the duke has never been kissed, however, Christabella forms the perfect plan. She can show him how to win a lady's heart and kiss him out of her system at the same time. But the problem with kisses is they often lead to something more, and soon, the only heart she wants him to win is hers.

Chapter One

Oxfordshire, 1813

*M*ISS CHRISTABELLA WINTER was in a terrible mood. A terrible, dreadful, horrid mood.

She cast a glance over her shoulder to make certain none of the guests at the country house party being hosted by her brother and sister-in-law wandered in the hall. Assured of her solitude, she crossed the threshold of the small, cozy salon where she had taken to hiding herself at Abingdon House. With its eastern-facing windows, generous hearth, and overstuffed chairs, it was the perfect place to indulge in an hour or two of uninterrupted reading.

She sighed as she closed the door at her back. Judging from the way her day had gone thus far, she may need a good three hours of pleasant diversion to distract herself from the grimness of her disposition. First, she deplored cold. Second, she did not like snow. Third, she was tired of playing charades, especially when none of the players could correctly guess what she was attempting to enact. Fourth, she had set her heart upon finding a wicked rake of her own at this cursed house party.

Instead, all the rakes had eyes for her sisters.

Which left Christabella with no one, the only hope of entertainment to be had in the small leather-bound volume she had secreted in the hidden pocket she had sewn into her gown for just such a purpose. Because the book she was about to read was not just any book. No, indeed. It was a volume in the forbidden, wicked, utterly bawdy series of books known as *The Tale of Love*.

On another sigh, she threw herself into one of the chairs by the hearth, plucking the book from her pocket. At least she was assured of some rakish diversion within the pages of her book, even if this house party had proven deadly boring thus far. She flipped to the page where she had last quit reading, toed off her shoes, tucked her feet underneath her bottom, and settled in.

That was when she heard it.

A noise.

The clearing of a masculine throat, to be precise.

She stilled, her eyes flying about the chamber.

And that was when she saw him.

The tall, golden-haired, infallibly handsome Duke of Coventry. The only man present at the house party who had yet to speak a word to her, not even during their introduction. He stood at the opposite end of the chamber, staring at her, his mien forbidding.

He looked, unless she was mistaken, as if he were vexed with her.

But how silly, for she was the one who ought to be nettled for the manner in which he was trespassing upon the salon she had claimed for herself. Why, it was all but her territory. He had no right to be here. None at all.

"Your Grace," she said, forgetting she ought to stand, slip her shoes back on, and curtsy. "What are you doing in my salon?"

His brows rose, as if he questioned her daring. But still, he said nothing.

What a queer man he was. Never mind that. He could

stand there all stoic and silent as he liked. She could talk enough for the both of them.

"Oh, very well," she said, frowning at him. "It is not *my* salon. But I have been reading here for the past few days, and I rather fancy it mine now. You will have to go somewhere else. Just look at how comfortable I have made myself in this chair. Do you dare disturb me?"

His nostrils flared. But still, he did not move. And still, he did not speak.

She wondered if it was because she had yet to observe formality.

"Must I curtsy?" she asked him. "It feels frightfully foolish to do so when we are the only two in the chamber. Just imagine us curtsying and bowing with no one to watch, when we are already committing an egregious faux pas by being here alone together."

His jaw seemed to harden, and his hands at his sides flexed. They were the only signs he was a man and not a statue fashioned of the coldest stone.

"Oh, very well." On an irritated sigh, she flounced her gown and rose to her feet. "I shall curtsy. But do not expect me to put my slippers back on. They are too tight. I think they belong to my sister Grace. Her feet are a bit daintier than mine."

She dipped into a mocking curtsy, holding his gaze all the while. "There. Are you satisfied now, Your Grace?"

Finally, at long last, his lips moved.

He spoke.

One word, curt and definitive. "No."

She pursed her lips, studying the aggravating man. "That was a perfectly acceptable curtsy, I will have you know. One does not need to wear slippers in order to curtsy."

"Do you always talk this much?" he asked then, quite

rudely.

She blinked at him. "I think I liked you better when you were silent, Your Grace."

Then, the strangest thing happened, right there before her. The Duke of Coventry smiled. And her heart kicked into a gallop. Good heavens, he was the most handsome man she had ever beheld when he smiled that way.

Until he quite ruined the effect by speaking once more.

"The feeling is mutual, Miss Winter."

Want more? Find Christabella and Gill's story, *Wild in Winter*!

Don't miss Scarlett's other romances!

(Listed by Series)

Complete Book List
scarlettscottauthor.com/books

HISTORICAL ROMANCE

Heart's Temptation
A Mad Passion (Book One)
Rebel Love (Book Two)
Reckless Need (Book Three)
Sweet Scandal (Book Four)
Restless Rake (Book Five)
Darling Duke (Book Six)
The Night Before Scandal (Book Seven)

Wicked Husbands
Her Errant Earl (Book One)
Her Lovestruck Lord (Book Two)
Her Reformed Rake (Book Three)
Her Deceptive Duke (Book Four)
Her Missing Marquess (Book Five)

League of Dukes
Nobody's Duke (Book One)
Heartless Duke (Book Two)
Dangerous Duke (Book Three)
Shameless Duke (Book Four)
Scandalous Duke (Book Five)
Fearless Duke (Book Six)

Sins and Scoundrels
Duke of Depravity (Book One)
Prince of Persuasion (Book Two)
Marquess of Mayhem (Book Three)
Earl of Every Sin (Book Four)

The Wicked Winters
Wicked in Winter (Book One)
Wedded in Winter (Book Two)
Wanton in Winter (Book Three)
Willful in Winter (Book Four)
Wagered in Winter (Book Five)
Wild in Winter (Book Six)

Stand-alone Novella
Lord of Pirates

CONTEMPORARY ROMANCE

Love's Second Chance
Reprieve (Book One)
Perfect Persuasion (Book Two)
Win My Love (Book Three)

Coastal Heat
Loved Up (Book One)

About the Author

USA Today and Amazon bestselling author Scarlett Scott writes steamy Victorian and Regency romance with strong, intelligent heroines and sexy alpha heroes. She lives in Pennsylvania with her Canadian husband, adorable identical twins, and one TV-loving dog.

A self-professed literary junkie and nerd, she loves reading anything, but especially romance novels, poetry, and Middle English verse. Catch up with her on her website www.scarlettscottauthor.com. Hearing from readers never fails to make her day.

Scarlett's complete book list and information about up-coming releases can be found at www.scarlettscottauthor.com.

Connect with Scarlett! You can find her here:
Join Scarlett Scott's reader's group on Facebook for early excerpts, giveaways, and a whole lot of fun!
Sign up for her newsletter here.
scarlettscottauthor.com/contact
Follow Scarlett on Amazon
Follow Scarlett on BookBub
www.instagram.com/scarlettscottauthor
www.twitter.com/scarscoromance
www.pinterest.com/scarlettscott
www.facebook.com/AuthorScarlettScott
Join the Historical Harlots on Facebook

Made in the USA
Monee, IL
13 April 2020